Mortem Obire

A Tennebrose Novella

Ashlyn Drewek

Fox Hollow Books

Cover design by Wolfsparrow Covers

To Halloween,
You were my first love.
You'll never know how much you mean to me.

A warning to the reader

This book includes references to and depictions of: off-page child sexual abuse and death; off-page child kidnapping; homophobic slurs; attempted sexual assault; violence and torture, including strangling, drowning, and weapons; PTSD and anxiety; alcohol use and drunk driving; and parental/caregiver death. It is intended for a mature audience and reader discretion is advised.

Chapter 1

Jamie

Piercing the needle through the chicken breast in front of me, I lined it up with the suture next to it, exhaling a slow, steady breath like a sniper preparing for their next shot. I was just about to hook it through the opposite side of flesh when something loud slammed against my door, followed immediately by frantic banging. The needle jammed into the chicken, way off its mark.

"Fuck!" I tore off my latex gloves and hurried to the door, debating whether or not I should try to grab a t-shirt on the way. Given what time it was, I decided I didn't give a shit about decency since I wasn't exactly expecting company. Peering out the peephole, I rolled my eyes at the obviously drunken idiot on the other side. "It's after midnight," I groaned, opening the door and stepping backward. "How did you even get past security?"

Larkin stumbled inside, grinning from ear to ear despite the fact he was covered in mud and grass stains. "Good, you're awake!"

"You didn't know that before—what the fuck happened to you? Why are you bleeding?" I grabbed his hands, both covered in blood and dirt, and brought them closer to my face. The right one had cuts all over his swollen knuckles. The left was similar but it was accompanied by weird red splotches on his wrist and a large gash across his palm. "Oh my God! What the fuck did you do? Did you get into another bar fight?"

He scoffed, his dimples popping as soon as he smiled innocently. "Come on! That happened *one* time and that homophobic dickwad deserved it."

Ignoring his dimples, I arched an eyebrow at him. "Then what happened this time?"

Larkin swayed closer, his dark eyes glassy. Tequila emanated from his breath as he answered in a conspiratorial whisper. "It was for you."

"*What* was for me?" I whispered back, curious and yet dreading his answer.

"I can't—oh, fuck! I didn't even bring it!" His face crumpled and he hung his head, his muscled shoulders slumping. "I was going to bring you a goose but the fucker bit me and flew away."

I tried not to laugh at how dejected he was but I couldn't help shaking my head at the same time. "And just how drunk are you?"

Larkin grinned again and pinched two fingers together. "Just a lil bit."

"Come sit down so I can look at this," I said with a sigh, directing him to the small kitchen table where my med bag was set up. The perks of being a nursing student, I guess, *and* being a senior. It meant I got to live in one of Tennebrose University's tiny apartments rather than a regular dorm room, giving me the space and privacy to patch up my injury-prone friends whenever they came knocking.

Shoving the chicken breast to the side, I pulled on a fresh pair of gloves and lowered the work lamp closer to Larkin's left hand to see what I was dealing with. The edges of the cut were clean, like it had been sliced open as opposed to torn. By what, I had no idea. Definitely *not* a goose. Maybe a broken bottle?

"A goose, huh?" I asked, soaking a wad of cotton squares with saline solution and dabbing at his hand.

"It was a big goose." Larkin leaned forward, watching me work with a fascinated expression. Frankly, I'd be surprised if he could see anything with how much tequila I could smell. For his sake, I hoped he ran here from wherever the hell he'd been and didn't park his SUV up the side of a telephone pole.

"Why were you trying to kidnap a goose?"

"For you," he replied, so quietly that I looked up to make sure I heard him correctly. His big brown eyes were suddenly serious behind the glaze of alcohol. "To keep you safe."

"I don't need a goose. I have you. My own personal attack dog." I was trying to lighten the mood, even though my heart thumped wildly in my chest. It had been ages since he'd looked at me like that and I'd be a liar if I said I hadn't missed it.

He swayed forward again, his head tilted. I thought he was going to kiss me, but sadly his mouth bypassed mine and he embraced me with one arm instead. Still, I relished it, feeling him against me, letting his body heat soak through his t-shirt and into my bare skin.

"I love you, man," he mumbled against my neck.

"I love you too. Now are you going to let me finish or not?"

He shook his head, tightening his hold around my neck. Even though I couldn't see it, I knew he was grinning.

"You're such a pain in my ass." I forcefully shoved him back in his seat and resumed bandaging his hand without much assistance on his part.

"I know." He expelled a sigh that sounded more than sarcastic. It sounded like genuine exhaustion had taken hold more than the sedative effect of the alcohol.

I finished quickly, wrapping gauze around his hand and tucking the tail into place so it wouldn't unravel. Retrieving a bottle of water from the fridge and some meds, I set them in front of him on the table. "Take these. And then you should get some sleep."

"But I'm not sleepy." He was back to being goofy, sticking out his lower lip and blinking up at me with the big, sad puppy eyes he'd perfected over the years. Those eyes, combined with his dimples, had let him get away with everything growing up—from teachers to girls to his overwhelmed grandmother. Larkin Galvan could do no wrong and he knew it.

"Well, I have to put this stuff away," I said, as if I could resist his charm more than anyone else. I'd been losing that battle for as long as I'd known him.

"S'ok if I just hang?" He didn't wait for an answer before he strolled to the couch and plopped down, snagging the remote from the end table.

"Yeah, sure. You know you don't have to ask."

After cleaning up the bloody leftovers from his hands and depositing the chicken breast back in the fridge for another night, I joined him on the couch. Since it was technically only a loveseat, there wasn't much room, especially with his thick thighs spread, taking up most of the space.

As soon I sat, he hooked the inside of my knee and dragged my leg over the top of his rather than scooting over.

I didn't mind, except for the fact his hand stayed where it was, casually draped along the inside of my thigh. Where his index finger touched bare skin instead of slinky basketball shorts, he drew tiny circles, almost absentmindedly.

I felt every one of them though, each one sending a jolt of electricity up my leg and straight to my dick. I tried to ignore it, but I couldn't. I was fixated on that one finger instead of whatever action movie he'd turned on.

He was drunk, that was all. And he was always fiddling with something in his hands. Pens, keys, whatever. It didn't mean anything. We'd grown out of that phase of our friendship years ago, the one where we experimented with each other as teens or got each other off out of boredom or frustration.

Besides, I'd rather deal with blue balls than more heartbreak at the thought Larkin would never be mine. Not in the way I wanted. I had to content myself with being his friend and nothing more. It was such a fucking cliche, anyway. Falling for your straight best friend. Even though, I'd been his first... everything. First kiss. First hand job. Blowjob. The only thing we hadn't tried was anal. But I hadn't tried that with anyone except the dildo I kept stashed in my nightstand. Maybe there was a stupid part of me that was holding out hope he'd be *that* first too.

I tried to subtly shift, angling my hips away from him to disguise the fact I was starting to pitch a tent right there for no goddamn reason other than the fact he was touching me.

His fingertips tightened on my leg, preventing me from getting far. "Where are you going?"

"Nowhere. Just trying to get comfortable," I lied.

Unconvincingly, since his gaze zeroed in on the very thing I was attempting to hide.

"I can help with that. If you want." His voice was low and husky, the scent of tequila wafting between us in the close space.

I should have kept my damn mouth shut. I should have thrown his hand off and gone to bed. I should have done a lot of things. But instead, I let my gaze slide to his. "Oh yeah?"

"Yeah." He gave me a slow smile, the light from the TV illuminating one of the dimples that I loved. "You helped me"—he held his bandaged hand up—"I can help you."

"I thought we were done with that?"

"We don't have to be."

"You know it's not good for..." *Me*, I wanted to shout, but ended lamely with, "Our friendship."

His fingertips drifted higher along my thigh, dragging the soft material with them and exposing more skin. Even the dusting of leg hair stood up, ready and begging for his attention. My whole body felt like it was charged with static electricity, waiting to discharge in one, massive jolt.

Either he was too drunk to hear me or too drunk to care because his hand continued to float northward, skimming along the crease of my thigh. The edge of his pinky grazed my sac and every muscle in my body tensed.

"Lark..." I swallowed thickly, desperate for him to stop but dying for him to continue.

Thanks to the angle of how we were sitting, his elbow pressed against my chest, keeping me flat against the couch as his hand snaked underneath the waistband of my shorts and his warm palm made contact with my cock.

"Freeballing," he murmured, more to himself than me. Still, I nodded dumbly, trying not to combust on the spot.

How long had it been since we'd done this? I couldn't even remember. I tried not to think about him like that. Tried, and failed miserably. I'd been jerking off to fantasies of him since freshman year of high school. And shit like this didn't help matters.

"You know," he continued softly, shifting closer and running his fingertips up and down my shaft, "you could always take these off."

"We shouldn't be doing this," I muttered in a weak protest as the pad of his thumb circled my crown, spreading beads of pre-cum around the tip.

"Why not?" When I turned to face him, trying to be the voice of reason, one look at his molten gaze snatched the words right out of my mouth. All I could do was stare at him while he patiently waited for an answer, teasing me with soft, slow strokes, knowing I would cave. I always caved.

"You're straight." It was the only thing I could come up with in the moment. I hated that it was my go-to answer, but it was the only one I had.

"Doesn't mean I don't know my way around a dick. Especially your dick." He fisted my cock and slid it up and down slowly, twisting at the crown the way he knew I liked.

"How many dicks do you know your way around?" I wasn't sure I even wanted to know the answer to that. As far as I was aware, I was the only one, but who knew what secrets Larkin kept from me, especially from living in one of the frat houses on campus. Sports might not have been a thing at Tennebrose, but "social organizations" aka: frats and sororities certainly were, along with the rumored secret societies.

He rolled his lower lip between his teeth, letting his gaze travel down my bare torso to where his hand was moving steadily beneath the swishy material. He clearly wasn't going to answer, which was both frustrating and humiliating.

I'd been in love with this man since we were kids, before I even knew what "gay" or "straight" meant. The thought of him with anyone else, girls and *especially* other guys, made my skin prickle. But then he shifted again, slipping his bandaged hand inside the leg of my shorts to tease my balls while his dominant hand stroked my shaft, and I forgot all the reasons I was mad at him. No, I couldn't have him in the way that I wanted, but I could have these moments with him even though I knew they were fleeting and would inevitably gut me along the way.

His left hand dipped between my cheeks, two fingers circling my rim and dancing over my taint as he continued jacking me off.

"Oh fuck," I groaned, thrusting against his hand before I could help it.

"Is that good?" he asked, his breath hot against my ear. I hadn't even realized he pressed his forehead against my temple until he spoke.

Nodding, I clutched the arm of the couch to keep from fucking his hand like a maniac.

He pulled his left hand out quickly and spit on his fingertips before diving back in. Smearing his saliva around my hole with the left, his right hand worked steadily on my shaft, stroking, squeezing, until I was practically panting and wriggling against him.

"Can I try something?" he asked.

I didn't trust myself to speak, so I nodded again.

The pad of his finger pressed against my hole. Slowly, inch by inch, he sank it inside of me. The slight burn, the pressure. The fact it was fucking Larkin? I moaned, grabbing onto his jean-clad thigh to try and keep myself here on Planet Earth.

"It's so tight," he whispered, crooking his finger inside. A burst of pleasure spiraled through me and I bit my lower lip, committing every sensation to memory while also trying not to come too soon.

His left hand might have been finger-fucking me slowly, but his right hand sped up, working the tip of my cock in fast, sure movements. I might have been trying to hold out, but he clearly had other ideas.

"You gonna bust?" he asked, his breathing nearly as ragged as mine, his own bulge unmistakable even behind the restrictive denim.

"Fuck yes."

"Good. I want to see it. Look at me."

I did as he said, forcing my lust-drunk gaze to meet his. That was it. The moment I locked onto his sultry brown eyes, I was done for. He drove his finger deeper into my ass and jerked my cock and the planets fucking aligned. My orgasm started somewhere in outer space and ripped through me, hurtling down my spine and straight to my balls. I unloaded all over the inside of my shorts, groaning and grunting and trying to keep my gaze on Larkin's as the waves of pleasure tried to swallow me whole.

"Goddamn," Larkin whispered, his gaze fixed on me with rapt attention. His tone sounded almost reverent, which would have made me blush if I hadn't already nutted all over him.

I was shaking by the time I was done, exhausted from fighting the morality battle within myself and from the aftermath of someone else giving me one of the best orgasms of my entire life.

Without speaking, he slid his hands out of my shorts carefully and reached for the box of tissues on the end table.

"Let me go get you a towel or something." I got to my feet, wobbled, and hurried to the bathroom to clean up quickly. After I changed into a fresh pair of shorts, I returned to the living room with a damp hand towel.

It was too late.

Larkin was asleep on the couch.

A twinge of disappointment shot through me. More than a twinge, if I was being honest with myself. What was I expecting though? To come back and find him naked, his thighs spread, waiting for me to deep-throat him into oblivion? And then we'd cuddle on the couch and fall asleep like we'd done countless times before?

I shoved the fantasy scenario back in its box and grabbed the throw blanket from the back of the couch, draping it over his torso even though I knew he'd kick it off in the middle of the night. Thanks to our many sleepovers over the years, I knew he was a hot sleeper. But he was also a snuggler and more than likely would wad it up and hold onto it like a person.

Wishing that person was me, I stumbled to my bedroom and flopped face-first onto my bed. I lay there for a moment, sulking about sexualities and friendships and crossed lines, before I realized I didn't have *my* sleeping partner, the one who wouldn't break my heart.

Grabbing a well-worn and well-loved stuffed goose from where he'd gotten wedged between the mattress and the headboard, I tucked him under my arm and exhaled a sigh. Mr. Goose was safe, which meant *I* was safe. To most people, it probably seemed ridiculous that a twenty-two-year-old needed a stuffed animal to go to sleep, but I did. It was one of the few things that kept my anxiety in check, especially this time of year.

The goose was a gift from Larkin when we were thirteen. He gave it to me before the ambulance took me away, *that* night, just after he'd saved my life. It was his prized possession, the only thing he had when he moved to our small New Hampshire town from a shadowy, unknown past in New Mexico.

I clung to it *that* night and every night after. They were both my guardian angels, one for the day and one for the night. And once a year, on Halloween, I was lucky enough to have both of them curled up in bed with me, keeping me safe. It was the only combination that kept the ghosts away.

I squeezed Mr. Goose tighter. Another horrible holiday was fast approaching. It seemed like yesterday was the beginning of the fall semester and now Halloween was two weeks away. I longed for the days when it used to be my favorite holiday, before it became my nightmare. But as long as I had Larkin and Mr. Goose, I'd be ok. I'd survived once. I'd survive again.

At least, that's what I told myself over and over until I fell asleep.

When I woke in the morning, Larkin was gone. The blanket was folded neatly on the end of the couch—the only evidence he'd ever been there.

Chapter 2

Larkin

Despite how creepy it might be to the majority of people, watching Jamie sleep was one of my favorite pastimes. It started when we were kids, when he'd have horrible nightmares, and it was something that carried on into our burgeoning adulthoods. The way his nose wrinkled, his fingers twitched, curling tighter around Mr. Goose—it was all so fascinating to me. By staying awake and watching over him I could stop the nightmares before they took hold. When his brow furrowed too long or he flinched too hard, I could take his hand and squeeze it tight and he'd settle again instead of waking us both up with terrified screaming.

But out of all of his expressions, I loved his sleepy smiles the most, when he was still somewhere between dreams and wakefulness. When he'd open his brilliant blue eyes and see me next to him and just... smile. It made my chest squeeze every single time.

These days, we didn't share a bed too often anymore. Unless I happened to pass out drunk around him, sleeping together was usually reserved for one night a year—Halloween. It was the only time Jamie let me in past the barriers he'd firmly installed in recent years, claiming it was "better" for our friendship. Except last night when I managed to give him a handjob.

The details were still kind of fuzzy, but I definitely remembered the way he moaned and bucked against my hand. The way he looked at me, the way his body felt, responding to everything I was doing. God, I wanted more of it. It might have been wrong and immoral and dirty, but I didn't care. I wanted it to be like when we were teenagers, before my grandmother caught us and made me swear to stop sinning against God and be the good Catholic she wanted me to be.

She was all I had, so I swore. To convince her—and myself—I was keeping my promise, I dated any girl who so much as glanced my way and dropped them the second I felt the pressure at home let up. I tried to make it work a couple of times, but when I kissed them, my mind always wandered to Jamie. He'd been my first kiss anyway. "Practice," or so we said. Just like we "practiced" handjobs and blowjobs, because *those* were important skills to have when dating girls.

I didn't know if Jamie could see through my bullshit or not, but he went along with it until one day he didn't. It all came to a screeching halt our sophomore year of college except for the rare occasions, like last night, when I could wheedle my way into his pants. I told myself I was doing it for him, to make him happy, but that was a lie. I was doing it for me. Even though it was "wrong," I fucking ached to touch him, to see that look in his eyes as he was engulfed in pleasure.

By morning, the guilt set in. Guilt for lying to my now-dead grandmother and for making Jamie break whatever boundaries he'd put into place regarding our friendship. It didn't stop me from watching him sleep, though, just for a moment, before slipping out of his apartment.

My hand still hurt like a motherfucker. Not from the goose bites, although those didn't feel pleasant either. No, the cut he'd bandaged came from a knife, though there was no way in hell I could ever tell him that. Just like I could never tell him why I slipped out before he was awake and why I was making the drive back to our hometown of Sunderland, to my grandmother's house, with a fresh roll of duct tape and heavy chains in the cargo area of my SUV.

On the outside, Grandma's house was the same as when she was alive—fall flowers bloomed in the window boxes and lace curtains hung in the darkened windows.

But inside, there was a secret. My secret. My horrible, hideous secret. One I hoped Jamie would never learn because it would ruin everything we'd both tried so fucking hard to forget.

Climbing out of the car, I grabbed my supplies and headed into the house, not bothering with any lights until I got to the top of the basement stairs. I flipped them on and unlocked the padlock on the basement door, jogging down the stairs.

Tied to one of the metal support posts in the basement with some old rope I'd scrounged up, the monster of my childhood sat with his forehead resting against the pole. A hulking beast with dark, greasy hair and a nasty scar on his cheek that cut through his unkempt beard. Yeah, he was big, but so was I. I wasn't the prepubescent weakling he'd spent years tossing around like a rag doll, a fact he'd learned the hard way when I beat the shit out of him and dragged him down here.

Picking his head up, he squinted against the harsh light. One of his eyes was practically swollen shut, dried blood crusted on the side of his face.

I hefted the handful of chains into view, giving him a dark smile. "I think it's time for an upgrade. Can't have any more escape attempts."

He snarled something behind the duct tape, but it was muffled.

Ignoring him, I secured the chains around his wrists and wrapped them as tightly as they could go, using a padlock to hook it all together. Since he'd already managed to free himself once, I left the original rope in place. Double bindings couldn't hurt. Unless he was fucking Houdini, he wasn't getting out again.

He mumbled something else, his open eye narrowed on me.

Rolling my eyes, I stepped forward and picked at the corner of the tape until I could rip it off halfway. "What?"

He sucked in greedy gasps of air for a moment, his sweat-stained shirt heaving with each breath. "What's your plan, kid? You can't keep me chained up forever."

"Not forever. Just long enough to get the cops everything they need to lock you up for good. Hopefully they extradite your ass to a state with the death penalty so I can watch you fucking die."

He barked out a laugh. "You think they're going to be ok with you holding me hostage? Vigilante justice don't fly, kid. Do you have any idea how many felonies you're committing right now? You're going to be in a cell right there with me."

I unsheathed the knife from the small of my back—the same one he'd pulled on me two days ago—and pressed it against his throat, bringing an immediate end to his laughter. "Or I guess I could always kill you and save the justice system a couple million."

He didn't even flinch. "You don't have it in you."

"It's not like it's hard. I watched you do it how many times? I lost count once we got into double digits."

"Then do it," he sneered. "If you think you have the balls."

We stared at each other, dark eyes mirroring one another and simmering with mutual hatred. It *wouldn't* be hard. Press the knife in and keep pushing... The blade was so sharp, it wouldn't take much pressure. It'd probably be like slicing through a pork tenderloin. And Jamie would be safe. Forever.

He lunged at me, snapping his teeth like a rabid dog.

I jerked backward.

His laughter turned to a hiss of pain. He pressed his cheek to his shoulder, like he could stop the blood flowing from his neck from where I'd inadvertently cut him.

Stumbling back a couple of steps, I staggered toward the basement stairs. Blood glistened on the knife. It wasn't much. It's not like I hit the artery. His shirt was doing a fine job soaking it up. It's not like it was gushing like a faucet, not like when he did it all those times before...

I hurried up the stairs and slammed the basement door shut, padlocking it again. Rinsing the knife off in the sink, I poured bleach down the drain, breathing hard, trying to inhale the fumes and get the stench of blood out of my nose. But how do you erase a memory? Memor*ies*? The smell of urine, the sound of screaming, pools of blood so thick it made the bottom of my shoes sticky.

I squeezed my eyes shut, forcing myself to think about Jamie. Jamie, who was warm and kind and funny. Jamie, who made me laugh and who listened when I talked and gave the best hugs. Jamie, my best friend. The one I would do anything for, even if it meant I killed the fucking monster in the basement. I didn't intend to, but if that fucker bled out down there, then so be it. The world would be better off. *Jamie* would be better off and that's all that mattered.

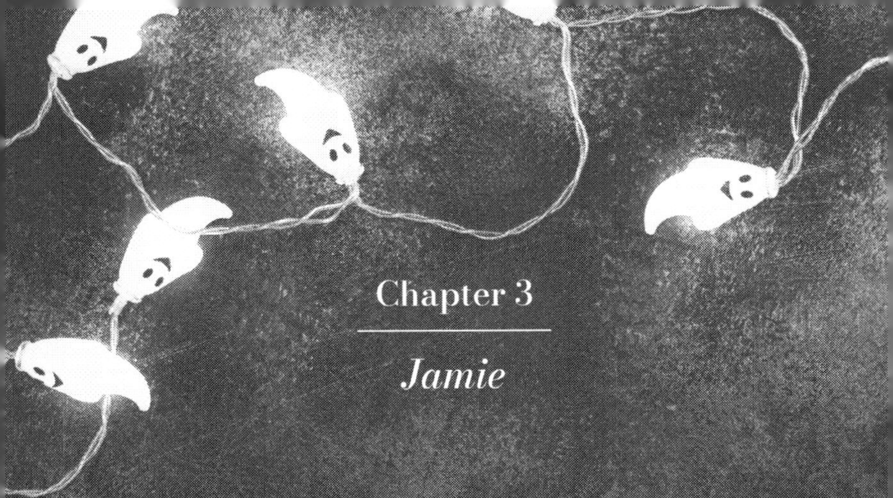

Chapter 3

Jamie

At night, Tennebrose always had a different vibe. A darker vibe. During the day, the historic buildings and flagstone walkways lent the university an old-world air of sophistication. It was quaint. Charming. Picturesque.

But in the dark, you'd swear things watched you from the shadows and ghosts whispered your name as you passed by. The place was haunted—everyone said so. But everyone always said that about old buildings.

I would have told myself it was stupid and childish, except I'd seen way too many ghosts on campus to dismiss it as a bunch of urban legends. And the closer we got to Halloween, the more restless those ghosts got. Just like me.

One October day in my freshman year, I almost had a full-blown panic attack in the middle of my biology class. I was already on edge simply because it was October, but then a ghost actually touched me and I lost my shit.

When Dr. Corbin pulled me aside after the lecture, I thought he was going to tell me to go see a shrink—something I'd already been doing since I was thirteen, with zero progress to show for it. The therapists said the "ghosts" I saw were all in my head, products of my anxiety and the PTSD from *that* Halloween manifesting themselves. By the time I got to Tennebrose, I'd learned to keep my mouth shut about the things I saw. I didn't tell anyone. Not my parents. Not even Larkin. I was already the nerdy gay kid who'd escaped a horrible death, I didn't want to be seen as even more of a weirdo, especially when Tennebrose was supposed to be my chance to start over.

Instead of patting me on the head or sending me to one of the university psychiatrists, Dr. Corbin rocked my world for the second time in my life.

"You're a medium, Jamie," Dr. Corbin said patiently as I paced back and forth in his office, shaking from head to toe, the feeling of the ghost's icy grip still circling my bicep. "You can interact with the spirit realm."

"This is bullshit," I said, shaking my head. "Some kind of prank you guys like to play on freshmen? Huh? Trying to get us in the Halloween spirit? I get Winslow is obsessed with witches and shit but I didn't sign up for this."

"Why do you think you're here?" He tilted his head to the side, watching me with the calm assuredness I imagined all world-class surgeons possessed. "You got a full ride to an obscure university you didn't apply to because we wanted you here. Tennebrose isn't just about training you for employment after you graduate. It's about giving you the skills you need to thrive in life and sometimes those skills involve things society doesn't tell you about, such as spirits."

My head was spinning faster than my spastic heartbeat. "Wh-what do you mean you wanted me here? How did you know? Were you following me? Because I haven't told anyone! Ok? No one! Did you get my files from my therapists? God, this is fucking crazy."

He smiled gently. "Some of my colleagues in admissions

have the ability to find prospective students like you. If we decide you have a gift worth exploring, we recruit you. It's as simple as that. And then once you're here, we wait to see if you even need our help before we try to reach out, to let you know you're not alone."

"Why? Why would you even care?"

"We find it's better to help students with their particular talents than let you wander through life, causing mayhem for the rest of us."

I flopped into the chair in front of him, sapped from the adrenaline crash and the strain of trying to process everything he was saying and *not* saying. "Rest of us? How many people are out there, like me?"

He considered it for a moment before shrugging. "It's hard to say really. There are those born with it and then there are those who develop it somehow, as you did that Halloween night."

I swallowed the lump in my throat. "You know about that too?"

Dr. Corbin nodded solemnly.

"Can you see them? The ghosts?"

He nodded again. "And don't worry, I'll make sure the classroom is warded properly before the next lecture so we don't have any more interruptions. Normally the facilities crew takes care of that sort of thing, but this particular spirit must have found an opening somewhere."

"What am I supposed to do when I see one? I try to ignore them, but some of them follow me. At first, it freaks me out, but then it gets annoying."

"The easiest thing is to tell them '*mortem obire.*' It translates to 'face death,' but we interpret it as a command to leave this life. It gives them permission to pass on."

"What if they don't go?"

"Then you tell me and I won't be as nice in my request," he said with a chuckle.

Although I walked out of Dr. Corbin's office feeling a hell of a lot better about my so-called "gift," I still didn't tell anyone. Not even Larkin. It's not that he wouldn't have understood or been supportive, but he already blamed himself for what happened when we were kids; I didn't want him heaping more guilt onto his broad shoulders. Ghosts were annoying and creepy, but armed with Dr. Corbin's words, I felt more in control than I had with years of meds and talk therapy.

Four years later, I'd used that Latin command countless times around Winslow. At the pharmacy. At the coffee shop. Definitely on campus. And it worked like a charm. One minute a silvery specter was floating nearby, staring at me like a dog begging for scraps, and the next they were gone, dissipating like mist.

So when I felt eyes on me as I headed toward my apartment after my nightly chem lab, I wasn't particularly alarmed.

Still, I slowed my steps and glanced around. The sidewalk around me was deserted. Closer to Dane Hall, the science building, I could see students milling about, but none of them were close enough to cause the odd sensation.

I turned in a slow circle, searching for the silvery glow that usually came with ghosts.

When my gaze settled on a figure across the street, standing behind a low stone wall, I flinched.

It was *him.*

The man who'd tried to murder me.

He was in the darkness between two of the wrought-iron lampposts, in the sliver of space where the pale yellow light didn't touch. His hateful gaze bore into mine, his lips twisted into a snarl.

It was the same look he had the night he tried to kill me, when his massive hands wrapped around my throat and squeezed until the world went black.

The feeling of being strangled all over again came rushing back.

My heart hammered against my ribs.

My vision blurred.

I couldn't breathe.

I forced myself to run—bypassing the sidewalk that would take me home and sprinting down the street toward Greek Row.

Larkin's massive frat house came into view and I ran faster, trying to outrun the panic. Outrun the stranger, whose stinking breath was hot on my neck, his outstretched hands just inches from grabbing me.

Sprinting up the porch stairs, I threw myself through the front door and slid to a halt in the foyer as thumping music and laughter assaulted me from every side.

There were people everywhere.

Fuck! They were having a party.

Raking my hands through my hair, I turned to go but a big hand clamped my shoulder. My yelp was mostly covered by the blaring music as I was spun around forcefully.

"Jame! My boy! You're here!" Larkin squeezed me in a bear hug but when I didn't return his enthusiastic greeting he sobered quickly. "What happened? What's wrong?"

"Nothing. I'm sorry. I didn't know you guys were having a party." I felt like the biggest fucking idiot in the world. There was no way I could tell Larkin about what happened, especially not when he was already buzzing.

He'd want to do something stupid, like go search the area for the guy—or call the cops, which is something I didn't feel like explaining to them. *Why yes, officer, the man who tried to kill me was just down the road. Yes, I'm sure. Mostly. Maybe. Well, it could have been a PTSD-driven hallucination. Please don't take me to the hospital.*

Larkin stuck out his plush lower lip. "Come on. Talk to me! What's going on?"

"Come on, man! Hurry your ass up!" One of his roommates, Cody, yelled from the living room, apparently mad that Larkin wasn't returning to their game fast enough.

"Hold your fucking horses!" Larkin snapped, turning back to me with a gentler expression. "Let's go to my room."

We made our way through the sea of bodies, up the stairs, to Larkin's room. Thankfully he had the foresight to lock it, which meant we wouldn't be interrupting anything.

"So what's up?" Larkin asked, ushering me inside and closing the door behind us.

Since he wasn't going to let it go and I couldn't come up with anything else believable at the moment, I opted for the truth. "He's here. I saw him." I didn't need to elaborate beyond that. He knew exactly who I was talking about. It was the same thing every year, ever since we were thirteen. I'd swear up and down I saw "him" out of the corner of my eye or on the street, but this time? I know for a goddamn fact I was staring at the man who'd tried to strangle me to death.

"That's impossible," Larkin replied, worry melting off his face with a relieved smile.

"No, I swear! I saw him on campus. Just now! Just... watching me."

"Jame, you know how you get this time of year."

"This isn't anxiety or fucking PTSD," I snapped, taking

a step closer, my jaw flexing. "I know what I fucking saw, Larkin! And it was him! Right in front of me! I don't know how, but somehow he found me!"

Someone crashed through the door and I yelped. Two drunk girls and a Neanderthal from one of the other frats on campus.

"Sorry," one of the girls slurred. "Didn't know it was occupied."

"Get the fuck out!" Larkin yelled, shoving them back through the door and locking it.

"I should go," I said quickly, heading for the same door that he'd just locked. Maybe seeing the Halloween stranger *was* all in my head. Or maybe it was some guy who kinda looked like him. Either way, it was impossible for my would-be murderer to have tracked me down at Tennebrose. He didn't know who I was, just like I didn't know who *he* was. That's what had made the whole thing extra terrifying—that some unknown person had nearly killed me and then disappeared. Every year I was convinced he'd come back to finish the job, like a bad horror movie, and every year Larkin tried to assure me that wouldn't happen.

"No, no, no, wait." Larkin slid in front of me, blocking the door and laying his hands on my biceps. "Just stay for a bit, ok? And I'll walk you home or back to your car or whatever. Give me, like, an hour for appearances. You shouldn't be alone right now anyway."

"I don't—"

He used all of his skills to transform into a giant, pouting puppy; big brown eyes, lower lip stuck out, hands pressed together entreatingly. I couldn't say no. Not to him. Not ever.

"Fine," I sighed.

When he grinned, his dimples popped, turning me into

mush. "Great! You wanna wait here or come down with me? Grab a drink? One drink. I'll get you the good shit in the fridge, promise. It'll help take the edge off."

"One drink. That's it."

Another flash of dimples, another flutter in the pit of my stomach. I was most definitely not in the mood to drink or socialize with other people, but I'd do it for Larkin.

We went downstairs and retrieved fresh bottles of beer from the fridge before rejoining the circle in the living room.

"About fucking time," Cody yelled when Larkin kicked a freshman named Tim out of an overstuffed recliner in the corner, resuming his seat from earlier.

I eased myself awkwardly into the room, trying to navigate the group gathered around the coffee table while looking for a place to lean.

Larkin snagged my belt loop and tugged me downward onto the extra-wide arm of the chair. He maintained a hold on the thin bit of fabric while I perched there, the heat from his hand radiating into the small of my back. I doubted anyone would have noticed with my t-shirt hanging in the way, but *I* knew it was there, a hot, steady point of contact.

"Truth or Dare," one of the girls said, zeroing in on Larkin now that he'd returned.

"Truth," he replied, taking a swig of beer from his bottle.

"What's the most embarrassing thing you've ever done?"

I held my breath, waiting to see what the answer was. Would I know the story he was referring to? Was I there when it happened? Larkin was a giant goofball wrapped in an endless supply of muscles and a megawatt smile. I'd never seen him get embarrassed a day in his life. He rolled with the punches like no one else and more than once I wished I could channel a fraction of his easygoing nature.

True to character, Larkin laughed and shrugged. "I don't know. I got my ass kicked by a goose the other night. So I guess that."

"What the fuck were you doing with a goose?" Cody asked.

"Thought I could catch it."

There was a chorus of laughter and people proclaiming he was an idiot.

"My turn," Larkin continued, turning to me with a sly smile. "Jame, truth or dare?"

"Oh, I'm not playing," I said, quickly taking a sip of my own beer.

The chorus turned on me next, booing and imploring.

"Come on." Larkin tugged my belt loop, gazing up at me. "One round."

I sighed. "Truth, I guess."

"What is the most useless piece of information you know?"

I couldn't help but laugh, relieved he didn't try to embarrass me. Not that *he* would have. He was too good of a friend. His roommates, however, weren't so nice, especially when they were drunk. "I don't know... um, that the smell of green apples and cucumbers can help with claustrophobia?"

"How the hell does that work?" one of the girls asked.

I shrugged, sipping my beer in lieu of answering. I wasn't the scientist, after all. I just read what I read.

"Ok, ok. Moving on from the truth shit. Who wants to do a dare?" another girl asked, rubbing her hands together mischievously.

"Me!" Cody said, his hand shooting up into the air. "Bring it on."

"Ok," the girl said slyly. "I dare you to kiss... him." Her index finger swooped around the circle until she ended, pointing at me. While I wasn't exactly out and proud, I wasn't totally in the closet either. But I guess in a circle of former jocks, I stuck out like a sore thumb as the obvious "other."

"I'll pass," I said quickly, throwing an apologetic look toward Cody. "No offense. You're not my type."

"Kiss him, kiss him, kiss him," the girl chanted, banging her plastic cup on the coffee table until other people joined in.

"Oh, come on," Larkin groaned. "What is this, high school? Show us the most embarrassing picture on your phone, bro. And no cheating."

"Dare's a dare, man," Cody said, standing slowly and spreading his hands. "Come here, pretty boy."

"I don't fucking think so." Larkin was on his feet so fast I barely had time to blink. I shot to mine as well, fisting a handful of Larkin's shirt between his shoulder blades before he could lunge across the narrow space.

"It's not worth it," I said quietly.

"What's your fucking problem?" Cody asked, squaring off with Larkin.

"You've had too much to drink and you're being a fucking dick," Larkin shot back. "You want to get the chapter shut down by harassing people at parties?"

"Give me a fucking break! You're just afraid your little boy toy might get off on it," Cody said, shooting me a nasty look.

"The fuck you call him?" If it was possible, Larkin got even bigger, rolling his shoulders back and broadening his stance like he was about to wrestle a bear—which wasn't far off from how big Cody was. Pretty sure I remembered hearing that he'd been a linebacker in high school and could have made a career out of it if he hadn't blown his knee out. Larkin played football too, but Cody was still bigger, especially now that most of his muscle had gone soft and unused.

"Your little boy toy," Cody repeated with a sneer. "Because everyone in this house sees how you two fucking look at each other, like you can't wait to slobber all over each other's dicks the second you get upstairs."

"One problem with your theory, Einstein. I'm not a fucking fag," Larkin snapped.

A wince shot across my face before I could stop it. I knew Larkin didn't mean it and I knew he didn't have problems with gay people, considering he'd spent most of his teen years coming to my defense from guys just like Cody. But it didn't take away the sting as that word sliced through the middle of me.

Almost as soon as the words left his mouth, Larkin turned, his lips parted like he wanted to say something else over the chorus of "Oohs" and nervous laughter.

I shook my head, warding off his apology, and swallowed the wave of unease roiling up the back of my throat.

"Let's get out of here," Larkin said quietly. Without waiting for me to say anything, he physically turned me around and steered me toward the door. His hand didn't leave the small of my back until we were through the front door and heading down the porch stairs.

Alone in the circle of light by the lamppost out front, Larkin pulled me to a halt again, his brown eyes glassy. "Jame, I—"

"You don't have to say anything," I said quickly, holding up a hand for effect.

"It's not like that," he whispered. "You know it's not."

"Then what's it like, Lark? You fucking kiss me and jack me off and everything else but God forbid anyone thinks you're a fag."

It was his turn to wince, squeezing his eyes shut like he was in physical pain. "Don't say that word."

"Why? Is *fag* suddenly offensive to you? Well, if it's so bad, why the fuck did you just say it?"

When he opened his eyes, they were even glassier—except it wasn't the alcohol. They were filled with tears. "Stop saying it. Please. Please, don't say it anymore."

I was struck by the plea in his voice, the desperate agony. This was more than his grandma's religious guilt weighing on him. Something else had happened, but I had no idea what. In front of Cody, for that split second, it was like he was a completely different person. Now the real Larkin was in front of me again and I was trying to reconcile the two of them.

"Will you tell me why?" I asked.

He shook his head, looking down at his feet, the muscles in his jaw flexing.

"Did something happen in New Mexico?" I ventured quietly.

He sniffed and blinked hard a couple of times, finally picking his head up but still refusing to look at me. After a moment, when it was clear he'd locked down whatever overcame him, he gave me one of his dazzling smiles, complete with dimples. "You want to swing by that cookie place on the way home? My treat."

I shook my head in defeat. I had my answer in a roundabout way—whatever demons Larkin had definitely came from his early childhood, but I'd be damned if I knew what they were. His time in New Mexico was the only part of his life that remained a mystery to me and it was beyond frustrating. He'd helped me so much over the years, had been an absolute rock for me, but he wouldn't let me return the favor. It hurt. But it also wasn't about me, so I tried to let it go.

"Yeah. Sure," I sighed. Since he wasn't going to open up, I might as well let him find comfort in fresh, baked-to-order cookies.

"So tell me more about the claustrophobia thing," he said as we started walking, his not-so-subtle way of getting the spotlight off of himself. "Green apples?"

"Yeah." I shrugged, trying to ignore the fact our arms brushed against one another every couple of steps. "I guess if you smell green apples or cucumbers then you think a space is bigger than what it is."

"Weird."

"Science."

"Science is weird."

"You're weird," I countered, giving him a light shove.

"Don't start with me, Kincaid!" He held up a finger in warning.

"Or what?" I shoved him again, this time a little harder.

"You know what." He shoved me back with a grin. "There's a reason I was the state wrestling champ two years in a row."

"Gotta catch me first." I shoved him backward and took off down the sidewalk. I might not have been a jock, but I'd always been able to outrun him, especially over any sort of long distance.

It didn't take long for the sound of his shoes hitting the concrete to catch up to me. I turned to see how much separation there was, alarmed to find he'd closed the distance quicker than I anticipated.

His arms wrapped around me from behind and we

careened off the sidewalk, falling into a massive pile of leaves that had been abandoned at the edge of a manicured lawn.

Laughing, I rolled over to look at him, noting I was still within the circle of his arms since he'd locked his fingers together to hold on to me. "Where did you come from?"

"I've been practicing my sprints," he replied with a laugh of his own. "Gotta be ready to chase bad guys, right?"

"Yeah. Nice tackle, by the way. Except I don't think the FBI tackles people. They're too dignified for that."

His arms tightened around me ever so slightly, his grin widening. "I don't think I'm applying to the FBI anymore."

I frowned at him. Joining the FBI had been his dream for as long as I could remember. He was obsessed with serial killers and vowed to stop as many of them as he could. What the fuck had happened to make him change his mind? "Why not?"

"You don't have any control over where you're assigned. And I want to be able to pick where I live."

"Where do you want to live?"

"Wherever you are."

I scoffed and tried to shove myself away from him. "You're an idiot."

He held on, keeping me close. "I'm serious. I need you in my life, Jamie. You're my best friend. The only person who really gets me."

"You can't give up on your dream job for me."

"I'd give up everything for you." His dark eyes shone in the moonlight, glittering like the night sky above. My heart thumped painfully, reminding me of all the reasons he would never be mine. As pretty as his words were, that's all they were.

"Larkin..." I touched his cheek before disentangling

myself from his arms so I could sit up. It was better if I wasn't looking at him, or touching him. I had more resolve when there was some separation between us. "You can't say stuff like that."

"But it's true." He sat up behind me but hung back, out of my line of sight.

"Don't you see how confusing this is? What happened back there with Cody makes it worse. You say and do these things in private that give me hope but when someone calls you out on it, you freak out. I can't do it anymore. It hurts too much."

"I never meant to hurt you." His hand slid over my shoulder and squeezed gently. He scooted forward, peering around me to try and catch my gaze, but I refused to look at him, to fall for his puppy eyes or his dimples again. "And I'm sorry if I have. You're the most important thing in the world to me. I love you, Jamie."

"That's the problem."

"What is?"

"You love me, as a friend, but I'm *in* love with you." I slid my gaze to his, bracing for the inevitable rejection. I never meant to blurt it out like that. It just happened. But now that I had, it was like ripping off a bandaid. Best to get the pain over with in one fell swoop than drag it out in small increments.

He didn't say anything. He didn't blink or smile or try to crack a joke. He just sat there, staring at me with wide eyes and a look of shock on his face. Did he really not know? Was he *that* oblivious? Or was the idea of me loving him so completely ridiculous it never even registered in his brain, because there was no possible way he'd ever reciprocate it?

"So maybe it's better if you followed your dream and joined the FBI to catch serial killers and I stay here in

Winslow," I continued quietly, turning my attention to the sidewalk before I imploded from embarrassment. "Dr. Corbin got me an internship with the fire department in the spring. If I like it, there's a job waiting for me after graduation. Or I'm sure I can go work at a clinic or something. Maybe even the hospital."

"You hate hospitals," he whispered, like he was still trying to comprehend everything I was saying.

"The point is, I have my life and you have yours and they're not the same."

"If you're staying in Winslow, then so am I."

"Lark, you're not listening to me."

"I am."

"No, you're not. I need space. I need to *not* be in love with my best friend." I glanced at him to make sure my words were sinking in. From the way his brow creased, they were, and my stomach twisted into guilty knots. "I'm sorry. I didn't want to hurt you. I'm not saying I don't want to be friends. You'll always be my best friend. I'm just saying we need better boundaries so maybe I can get over you one day."

"Whatever you need, Jame," Larkin said, his voice rough. He refused to look at me and the muscle in the side of his jaw flexed again in the moonlight, like he was physically biting back whatever he really wanted to say.

"Thank you." Out of habit, I started to reach for him but pulled my hand back quickly. "I'll talk to you later."

He didn't say anything as I stood and brushed the damp leaves off my clothes. Nor did he speak as I took a tentative step down the sidewalk, putting more and more distance between us. My heartbeat pounded in my chest as I left the circle of light cast by the streetlamp and crossed into the darkness. Balling my hands at my sides, my head whipped back and forth, checking trees and hedges for any sign of danger in the shadows. As soon as I entered another pale yellow circle of light, I exhaled a shaky breath. In the daylight, my apartment seemed so close to Larkin's, but at night? It may as well have been at the end of the earth.

I was a block away when the leaves rustled. I turned, expecting to see him jogging to catch up, to try and smooth things over, but he was headed in the opposite direction, his shoulders rounded and his hands shoved in his pockets.

My heart squeezed painfully at the sight of him. I wanted to run to him and throw my arms around him, to tell him I took it all back, that things didn't need to change. But the rational part of me knew they had to. I couldn't stay in love with a man who could never love me in return, not in the way I wanted. Since we were in our senior year, on the brink of starting our new lives, it seemed as good a time as any to make a clean break. I just wished it didn't hurt so fucking much.

Chapter 4

Larkin

I *need space.*

Jamie's words echoed in my head, stinging like a thousand cuts.

I can't do it anymore.

I slammed my palm against the steering wheel, again and again, until the pain ricocheting up my arm overwhelmed the pain clawing through my chest.

God forbid anyone thinks you're a fag.

"Fuck!" I screamed it at the top of my lungs until they burned.

Speeding through the darkness, my SUV hurtled toward my grandma's house and to the monster in the basement.

He had ruined everything. He *always* ruined everything. And he came back to do it again, one last time. But *this* time it ended. I would make damn sure of that. He almost took Jamie from me once before. There was no way in Hell I was going to let him do it again.

Slamming the car into park, I bolted up the porch steps and shouldered open the front door. Grabbing a knife from the butcher block on the counter, I made my way to the basement, careful of any movement I saw out of the corner of my eye.

Jamie said he saw him earlier on campus, but there's no way. No fucking way! Not unless the fucker got out again. I thought I'd kept him too weak to do that, though. Weak and helpless, like he'd kept his victims. No food and just enough water to keep his miserable heart beating while I searched the area for his truck and the little treasure trove inside. Between the stacks of polaroids and a well-worn map of the US with tiny red dots indicating where the bodies were, I'd finally have enough to hand him over to the police and put an end to this fucking nightmare once and for all. But there *was* another way to end it.

I tugged the light chain overhead and the single bulb clicked on, illuminating the beast before me.

As the circle of pale light swung back and forth, I could see he was decidedly gray. Corpse gray. His dark eyes bugged out and his mouth hung slack, a puddle of brown liquid pooling where his face had smashed against the concrete floor.

I nudged him in the ribcage with my boot. The heavy body was solid and he didn't react.

Kicking him harder, the corpse barely rocked.

He *was* dead.

He was dead!

The monster... my father.

I fell to my knees next to the body, knife still in hand. I wanted to weep for joy and scream in anger. He wasn't supposed to die in the basement. He wasn't supposed to get the easy way out. He was supposed to go to prison and suffer, like he'd made his victims suffer. He was supposed to get a fate worse than death because that's what sick fucking pedophiles like him deserved. Other criminals were supposed to chew him up and spit him out for the rest of his life and even then it wouldn't be a fraction of what he deserved.

Rage swelled within me, swift and sudden. I lunged out with the knife, sinking it into the side of his neck. The blade came away with a minimal amount of blood since it had already thickened in his veins. I wasn't the least bit satisfied.

I stabbed him again. And again. Unleashing a lifetime of fear and hatred against the shell of the man who'd fathered me, stolen me, and made me part of his twisted fucking games.

"Look at all these little toys to play with," he'd say when he brought me to parks and playgrounds, his arm around me affectionately like a doting father. "Go pick out your favorite. See if they want to play."

In the dark, when I'd cry for them—for myself, for a vague memory of a mother that faded a little more each day —he'd fall back on his usual threat. "Stop crying! Only little fags cry. You're not a fag, are you? Because you know how I feel about that... The only good fag is a dead one."

Bile rose in the back of my throat, threatening to choke me, along with the tears I couldn't stop now that they'd started falling, splattering all over the basement floor.

For ten years, I'd never had a single friend because the monster killed them all. I didn't know what a real friend was supposed to be until a knobby-kneed boy with bright blue eyes and dark, shaggy hair came up to me at school—another novelty in my fucked-up life—and introduced himself.

"Hi, I'm Jamie. Do you want to be friends?"

I need to not be in love with my best friend.

Jamie.

The boy who breathed life into me. Who taught me how to laugh. Who gave and gave and gave, asking nothing in return. I loved him so much that my chest hurt. I'd *always* loved him.

"Unacceptable, Larkin," Grandma's voice echoed through the basement. "Boys don't touch each other like that. It's sinful. Do you want to end up like your father? What would your mother say if she were still here?"

Squeezing my eyes shut, I ground the heels of my hands into my eyes, trying to shut out all the voices ringing in my ears.

You're not a fag, are you? the monster sneered.

Do you want to end up like your father? Grandma tsked.

It hurts too much, Jamie whispered.

The pain in Jamie's eyes when he said that fucking gutted me, because *I* did that to him. I'd lied to him, over and over, and kept him at arm's length even though I was the one who swore nothing would ever harm him again. I convinced myself he would be better off with some other guy, one who wouldn't bring monsters into his life, who *wouldn't* hurt him. He deserved someone who could love him openly and wholeheartedly, without fear of reprisal.

But the nightmare was over now. It was dead and rotting in front of me, which meant I could do better for Jamie. I could *be* better because the monsters keeping us apart were dead and gone. I was finally free. Just as soon as I got rid of the body.

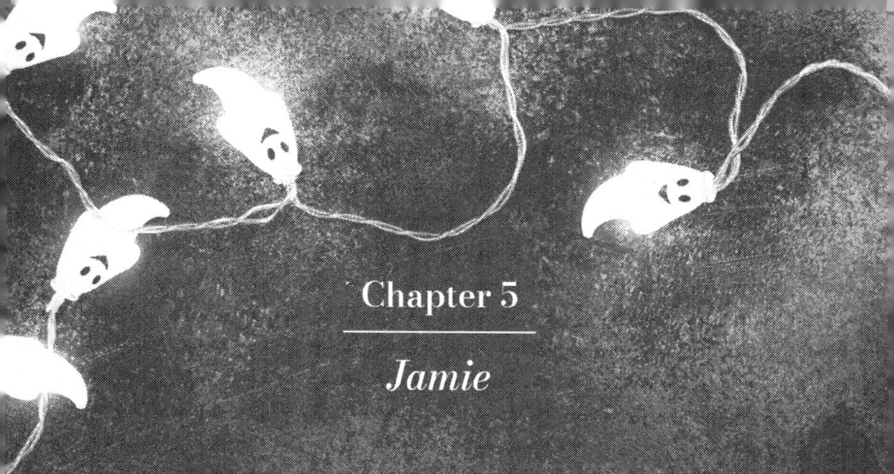

Chapter 5

Jamie

Going back to Larkin's the day after I told him I needed space wasn't my best move, but I forgot my backpack there the night before and I kinda needed that for class. Since he wasn't answering my texts, I figured I'd get one of his roommates to let me in and grab it and be on my way.

Sure enough, Tim, one of the newer pledges, didn't even blink when I said I needed to get my bag.

"Yeah, no problem," he said, pushing the door open wider.

"Thanks. Do you know where Larkin is, anyway?"

"No clue. His car was gone this morning."

"Ok. Thanks." I darted up the stairs and into Larkin's room. The bed looked like it had yesterday; two pillows and a blanket more or less thrown over the mattress, though half of it was pooling on the floor. It was his version of making the bed, something I'd chided him about when I thought he was planning to join the FBI. Ignoring the fact he'd apparently changed the entire trajectory of his life without telling me, I focused on the pillows. One was for his head and the other was for him to hold onto. Except, neither looked like they had been slept on or squished. Had he not come back last night? It was already late afternoon. Where the hell was he?

Guilt gnawed at me as I snatched my bag off the floor. My cell phone rang, too loud in the surrounding silence, making me flinch.

Larkin.

I answered hesitantly. "Everything ok?"

"Yeah. Sorry. I just saw your messages." He was breathing hard, like he'd been out running or lifting weights, though I didn't hear the usual metallic clanging in the background. Even if he was at the gym, he used his phone for music, which meant he would have known I was texting. So either he was lying or he didn't have his phone until just now, which still begged the question—where was he?

"Anything you want to talk about?" I asked.

"Uh, no. But I can meet you at the house in like two hours, if that's ok?"

"Don't worry about it. I'm here now. Tim let me in."

"Are you going to hang out until I get back?"

"I wasn't planning on it."

"Please?" I could already picture his puppy eyes and his downturned lip. "I want to see you. I don't like the way our conversation went yesterday."

A sigh escaped before I could help it. So he *did* want to talk, but not on the phone. Where the hell was he, anyway? Sunderland was about two hours away. Had he gone back to his grandma's house to finish packing her things? Without me? I mean, it's not like he needed my permission. It was technically his house, after all, and I'd literally told him the night before that we were leading separate lives, so it's not like I could be mad he was moving on with his. I just thought he'd want the help tackling decades' worth of antiques and knick-knacks.

"Two hours?" I repeated, checking the time on my phone.

"Give or take. Just hang out in my room. See if you can beat that level in Call of Duty. I'll be there as soon as I can."

"Fine. I'll see you in two hours." I disconnected and then flopped on his bed, kicking off my shoes. I wasn't really in a gaming mood, so I scrolled through my phone in an attempt to pass the time and not think about whatever the hell Larkin was up to. Without me.

I must have dozed off because the next thing I knew, there was a knock on Larkin's door, jarring me awake.

"Yeah. Coming." I sat up and scooted to the edge of the bed, wriggling my feet back into my shoes. The door opened and closed, but the boots that stopped in front of me didn't belong to Larkin. It's not like he'd knock on his own door, anyway.

I looked up slowly, swallowing when I saw Cody looming over me. "'Sup, man? Larkin's not here."

He smirked. "I know. Tim said you were up here, all alone."

"What do you want?"

"Call it unfinished business."

I couldn't help but shudder. I hated that term. Usually it was because it was in reference to ghosts, but it applied to this asshole, too. Still, I forced myself to my feet and headed toward the door. "Look, I'm not interested in whatever—"

Cody slid to the side, blocking me. "What's the deal with you two? You fuck buddies?"

"No," I managed to spit out, even though my heart was lodged in my throat. The door handle was right there, but even if I managed to grab it, I'd still have to make my way around his massive body somehow. "He's a friend. We grew up together."

"But you're gay, right?"

"What the fuck do you care?"

He trailed a finger down the side of my face before grabbing my jaw and pulling me closer. "You're no different from all the other slutty twinks that hang around here. You know that? I bet you suck Larkin's dick every chance you get. Hmm? Take his fat cock up that little ass of yours?"

"If you're so obsessed with Larkin's dick, why don't you go find him and leave me the fuck alone?" I tried to push him off but Cody was too strong. I was trapped, all over again, unable to save myself despite the fact I was a fucking adult this time around.

His face twisted into a sneer, all too reminiscent of another predator I wished I could forget. "I love mouthy little brats. It's going to be so much fun to bend you over your boyfriend's bed and listen to you scream like the bitch you are."

Mentally, I wasn't there anymore. I wasn't in Larkin's room. I was thirteen years old, back on the dark sidewalk in Sunderland, my Halloween mask obscuring most of my vision. All I could feel was that giant hand on my jaw, squeezing and dragging me closer, while hot breath wafted over my skin in the frigid October air.

"Are you going to scream like a little bitch?" the stranger's deep voice asked, squeezing harder until I cried out. "Go ahead. It's Halloween. No one will take you seriously. It's all fun and games tonight. You'll see."

I tried to kick and punch at the man that held me, swinging wildly as if I had a chance of escaping.

The stranger laughed at all of my attempts. He must have been twice my size. His meaty fingers dug deeper into my skin, never flinching from my pathetic attacks, until I realized with a sickening horror that they weren't on my jaw anymore. I'd been too distracted by my attempts to free myself to realize he'd managed to wrap both hands around my throat and was squeezing mercilessly.

My mask slipped and I caught a glimpse of his face. Dark, ugly, domineering, with a big scar on his cheek. It was seared into my memory for the rest of my life—however long or short that might have been. A combination of tears and black-and-white speckles blurred across my vision. My lungs burned from a lack of oxygen. I tried to scream for help, but all I managed was a pitiful squeak.

This end of the road was dark. No street lights. Normally Larkin and I loved it, loved the obscurity the darkness gave us, but tonight? I wished he'd met me at my house instead—there was a streetlight in my front yard. This stranger wouldn't have dared to step foot in such a brightly lit space. Larkin could have been waiting for me in the circle of yellow light, versus me, waiting for him on the cracked, uneven sidewalk while he ran back inside to get his bag for our last year of trick-or-treating.

The flickering jack-o'lanterns on his grandma's front porch watched as I crumpled to the ground, the man's oversized hands strangling the life out of me. Their orange grins seemed to relish my fate. A fitting spectacle for the darkest, most haunted night of the year—the murder of a thirteen-year-old boy in quiet suburbia by a total stranger.

An inhuman yell rang out in the distance, sounding above the fading heartbeat in my own ears.

Larkin's face was the first thing I saw—then and now. Like a light in the darkness, I latched onto it and refused to look away even though the sight was terrifying. Pure wrath darkened every line on his face, twisting it into a mask of savagery. His perfect white teeth were bared in a snarl and his dark eyes, usually so soft and warm, were as hard as onyx.

Now, just like when we were kids, I watched everything in slow motion, through a fog, as Larkin grabbed Cody by the back of his shirt and swung him around, throwing him into his desk. The larger man landed hard, knocking over the lamp and scattering desk supplies everywhere.

But that wasn't enough.

Larkin threw himself after his opponent and landed on top of him, straddling Cody's chest on his knees. His fist flew, again and again, punching the same bloody spot on Cody's face until it swelled and ceased to be recognizable as anything human.

Finally, Larkin yanked him up one last time, whispered in his ear, and slammed him into the floor so hard a framed picture of the two of us teetered and fell, the glass smashing on the floor.

Larkin appeared in front of me again, just as he had that night, breathing hard, covered in specks of blood that weren't his own. "Are you ok? Did he hurt you?"

Unable to find my voice, I shook my head.

"Let's get out of here." He slung a heavy arm around my shoulders and guided me out the door. Clinging to his shirt, I leaned against him, hoping some of his usual body heat would chase away the numbness.

Larkin's frat brothers eyed us with a mixture of curiosity and concern as we descended the stairs, but no one asked what happened or where Cody was. Maybe fist fights were common in their dwelling. It didn't really matter. By the time we reached the front door, the fear in my body had been replaced with pure humiliation. It only got worse once the murmured questions started, while others speculated what had happened.

Maybe he wanted it? And Larkin got pissed.

Cody's a fucking asshole. No one wants that.

Larkin's a fucking psycho when it comes to that dude.

Fucking fags.

I stole a glance backward, trying to determine who said the last one, but it was almost impossible with twenty-something guys standing around in little clusters. Larkin must not have heard since he calmly opened the door and stepped outside instead of turning around and beating one or all of them to a bloody pulp.

"Lark—"

"I'm taking you home," Larkin said, marching me straight to his SUV and opening the passenger door.

I slid into the front seat and turned toward him, a slew of questions and apologies on the tip of my tongue, but he closed the door in my face, literally and figuratively.

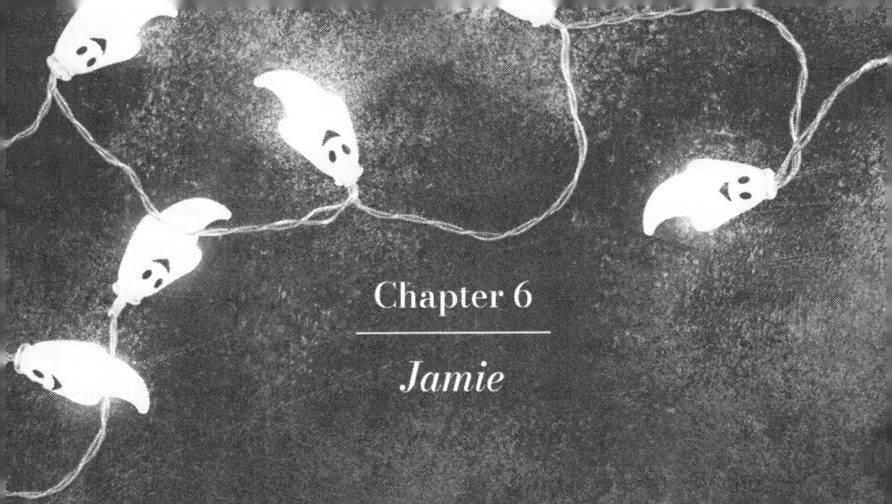

Chapter 6

Jamie

"What was that about back there?" I asked, dabbing carefully at Larkin's bruised knuckles with a cotton ball. I'd already cleaned the blood off his face and now it was time to deal with his hand since the ice pack finally brought the swelling down.

We hadn't spoken the whole way back to my apartment, though Larkin had managed to keep a hand on me almost the entire time—on the back of my neck, mostly, like he was afraid I might suddenly vanish if he let go.

He glanced up, sullen and deadly serious. "He shouldn't have grabbed you like that."

"You could have killed him," I murmured.

"Would that be such a bad thing?"

I paused, trying to decide if he was joking or not. From the hard line of his mouth to the way his eyes had narrowed, I could tell he wasn't. "Is he a piece of shit? Yeah, Lark. Definitely. Does that mean he deserves to die?" I shrugged helplessly. "I don't know."

"I do. And if he even *looks* at you again, I'll fucking end him."

"Easy killer."

"I'm serious." He took my hand in his until I met his gaze again. "As long as I'm around, I'll do whatever I have to to keep you safe. I mean that, Jamie. I've always meant it."

I tried to ignore the fact Larkin was running his thumb along my knuckles, another one of those little gestures that gave me butterflies. "You already saved me once. You don't have to keep doing it your whole life. It's not your fault some psycho came after me back then and it's not your fault one of your frat brothers is a pervy piece of shit."

He shook his head, his dark gaze dropping but not quick enough to hide the fact his eyes had welled with tears. "It *is* my fault, though."

"What are you talking about?"

"He only came after you because of me," he whispered, still not looking at me.

"Who did? Cody?"

Larkin shook his head again.

My mouth ran dry. "You mean th-the stranger? On Halloween?"

That time he nodded. Barely. "It's my fault. I'm so sorry, Jame."

"It's not your fault. The cops never even found him. No one knows who he was. Just some... psycho that you scared off by bludgeoning him with that flashlight."

"I have to tell you something." He picked his head up, but it took a couple of seconds for his gaze to reach mine. "Please don't hate me."

My stomach dropped, as much from his words as from the anguished expression on his face. "What is it?"

Swallowing thickly, Larkin drew in a steadying breath before answering. "He wasn't a stranger. He was there because of me. You see, he used to use me to lure other kids in. They'd follow me, back to him. And then he'd kill them. Right in front of me."

I stared at him, slack-jawed, trying to remember how to breathe while my brain went into overdrive, attempting to process everything he said. My own words refused to form any sort of coherent thought or even a question.

Larkin kept going anyway, now that the dam had been broken. "After the last one, in New Mexico, I guess I wouldn't stop screaming. I don't know why. I don't remember what happened. I've blocked a lot of it out so all I have are these bits and pieces. But he left. Left me *there*, with the corpse of a boy he'd kidnapped a couple of days before. The neighbors called the cops because of all the noise. That's where they found me, in the basement of some crackhouse, with that other kid. Or what was left of him...

"The cops ended up tracking down my grandma in New Hampshire. We'd been on the run for years, always moving, hiding from my mom and the cops. She died while I was gone, so it was just me and Grandma. And then I met you. And things were good. Until he came back that Halloween when we were thirteen.

"He'd been watching me—us. He wanted me to come with him again and when I didn't, he said I'd be sorry. Later that night he came after you. Because of me. If I'd just gone with him, none of this would have ever happened. I'm so sorry, Jamie. Please forgive me." His voice broke as the tears spilled down his cheeks, dripping onto the tops of his knees.

I finally managed to find my voice for one question. "Who was he to you?"

"My father."

I wanted to throw up. I wanted to scream. But more than anything, I wanted to comfort my best friend.

Pulling Larkin closer, I wrapped my arms around him,

breathing in the scent of sea salt and limes from his body wash, grounding myself in his familiar warmth. "It's not your fault," I whispered. "None of this was your fault, Larkin."

"He almost killed you," he sobbed against my neck, squeezing my ribcage so hard I winced. "And it's all because of me!"

"No, it's not. Listen to me. You *saved* me, Larkin. You stopped him. Ok? It's not your fault. I don't blame you for anything."

"I should have told you sooner. I know I should have, but I didn't want you to hate me. After everything that happened, I couldn't lose you. I'm so sorry."

I touched his cheek gently, wiping away his tears with my thumb despite the fact they continued to spill out. "You don't have to apologize. I don't blame you for what happened or for not telling me. I don't blame you for anything. Ok?"

"You don't?" He sniffed, his lower lip quivering.

I shook my head, smiling softly. "No. I don't."

"You don't hate me?"

"I could never hate you, Lark. Ever."

"You mean that?"

"Yeah, I do. I mean, kinda hard to hate you when I've been in love with you since we were teenagers." There. I said it. Twice in the span of two days. There was no taking it back, no way of saying I was only kidding. One of my biggest secrets was out there, in the open, and it was up to Larkin to decide what to do with that information.

Wordlessly, he slipped his hands around my waist and hauled me into his lap. Before I could ask what the hell he was doing, he wrapped one hand around the back of my neck and brought my mouth down to his, kissing me hard.

I shouldn't have kissed him back. Not like this. Not when he was upset and clearly trying to distract himself. But I had no self-control or self-respect when it came to him. I was greedy and I'd take whatever part of him I could, hoping it would be enough to sustain me. And maybe now that we'd cleared the air, things would be different.

It wasn't long before my dick hardened behind my zipper, straining painfully. I shifted my hips, trying to alleviate some of the discomfort, and inadvertently ground against Larkin's hard-on. He moaned against my lips and a bloom of heat surged through me. I did it again, harder, loving the way his fingers tightened on the back of my neck and his tongue dove even deeper into my mouth.

He broke away suddenly, tearing my shirt over my head and tossing it to the side. Instead of resuming our frantic kiss, he pressed his lips to my throat and worked his way down my chest, peppering my skin with kisses and small bites. When he got to my nipple, his tongue flicked out, making my toes curl. He repeated it on the other side slowly, drawing out the sensation while his hands grabbed my hips and pulled me down on his cock, rocking himself against my ass.

"I want your cock in my mouth," I said, running my fingers through his dark hair.

His gaze darted back to mine, wary and hopeful at once. "Yeah?"

I nodded, slipping out of his lap and dropping to my knees. I caught my lower lip between my teeth as I reached for his pants, glancing between the zipper and his eyes to make sure he was still on board. I mean, I assumed he would be. He'd always been ok with the idea of us "practicing" on each other when we were younger, preparing for our "real" relationships down the road, never mind the fact that Larkin's excuse was feeble at best. But in all the years I'd known him, he'd never turned down a blowjob. At least not from me.

Sliding his pants and his boxers down his hips and along his muscled thighs, I exhaled when his cock sprang to attention. Just like the rest of him, it was absolute perfection. Dipping down, I dragged my tongue along his length, from his balls to the tip, curling my tongue to gather the first traces of pre-cum.

Savoring the taste of him for a moment, I sucked on the head before swallowing him down. My mouth slid all the way to the base, not stopping until his cock was buried in the back of my throat.

"Oh, fuck, Jamie." He held either side of my head lightly, his fingers tightening and releasing in my hair, like he wanted to shove me down even farther but was holding himself back.

Easing myself back a bit, I bobbed up and down before deep-throating him again, taking him as deep as I could. When he squirmed beneath me, panting, I pulled back slowly, sucking hard all the way to the tip.

"That feels amazing," he sighed, his thighs flexing every now and again.

Pleased with the fact he was enjoying himself, I decided to take it up a notch. Adding my hand to the mix, I stroked his shaft while I continued to swirl my tongue around the head of his dick, licking and sucking his crown like a Chupa Chup.

"Take your cock out," Larkin said, running his fingers through the top of my hair and down the back of my head. "I want to watch you play with it."

Heat flooded my cheeks, but I did as he instructed.

Sliding my pants down to my knees, I sat back on my heels and gave my aching dick a few lazy strokes.

Larkin fisted his own cock, timing his movements with mine, watching my hand with rapt attention. "Just like that."

"Like this?"

"Yeah."

"What about this?" I shifted forward on my knees again and sucked his dick into my mouth.

"Shit, yes."

Even though Larkin had taken over jerking himself off, I kept my mouth sealed around the crown of his dick, sucking and licking as his strokes allowed. My cock throbbed in my hand as I spread pre-cum along my shaft while my other hand gripped my balls, squeezing now and again to stave off the budding orgasm. I didn't even need him to touch me—I could get off just by giving him a blowjob, but I didn't want this to be over before it even started.

"Do you want to go to your room?" he asked, running his fingers through my hair again and gripping a handful to tip my head back, making me pop off the end of his cock.

"Sure." A bed was infinitely more comfortable than the kitchen chair/floor situation we were currently in, but I didn't want to sound too eager in case he took it the wrong way.

I stepped out of my pants, leaving them in the kitchen, while Larkin led the way to my room, still dressed for the most part.

Once he was there, however, he shed his clothes in record time and enveloped me in another possessive kiss that left me weak-kneed. His body, defined from years of wrestling and football, was scorching hot in terms of looks *and* temperature. In the perpetually chilly dorms, being pressed against him was a relief. It was like having my own personal space heater.

Still kissing me, he wrapped his arms around my waist and maneuvered me backward to the bed. I scooted back to lay across the middle, but he shook his head and tipped his chin toward the pillows. "Up there."

Furrowing my brows, I nevertheless complied. We weren't usually pillow people. All the other times we'd messed around had been strictly middle-of-the-bed territory. Or the floor. Or random spots, like the couch or in a car, or even the cornfield next to his grandma's house. Pillows implied a level of intimacy that had never factored into our experimentations—if that's what you could even call this.

Once I was in position, Larkin crawled on top of me, his body stretching out over mine until I was practically dwarfed by him. He pressed his lips to mine again but this time it felt different. Less urgent. More intimate. It was the damn pillows.

As much as I was probably going to hate myself, I pushed against his chest gently as I broke our kiss, my brows furrowed once more. "Are you ok?"

"Yeah. Why?"

"You just seem... different all of a sudden." What else was I supposed to say? That it felt like instead of just letting me suck his dick and calling it a night, Larkin seemed like he wanted to "make love" to me? That was a mood killer, no matter how you put it.

"I want you, Jamie," Larkin said softly, caressing my cheek. "I'm tired of lying to both of us. I've never wanted anyone as much as I want you."

On the one hand, my heart leapt for joy because my childhood dream was coming true. On the other, I couldn't help but question the timing of it all. Generally, if something seemed too good to be true, it was. Between the conversation last night and what he told me today, I couldn't help but feel this whole thing was a last-ditch effort to try and keep things the way they were and not face reality.

"What happened to you last night? And where were you today?" I asked, studying his face for the truth.

He sighed and let his gaze drift to the side. His hand fell away from my face, but he didn't move to get up.

"Is this about what I said last night? About our lives going different places?" I continued, mindful to keep my tone neutral. After he'd finally opened up about his past, I didn't want to push him too much and run the risk of him shutting down—or shutting me out. Even though I'd initiated the blowjob, I didn't think it would go beyond that. I certainly didn't imagine pillows would be involved.

"I thought this was what you wanted. I thought... You don't want this?" His dark brows drew sharply over his eyes, but he looked more hurt than angry, like *I* was rejecting *him*, which was laughable. In all of my fantasy scenarios, I never imagined Larkin as the heartbroken one. Ever.

"Of course I do," I said quickly, running my fingers through the short hair at the nape of his neck. "It's what I've *always* wanted. But not like this. Not when you're clearly dealing with something. I mean, Cody. Your dad?" I had to force myself to spit out the last word. "Jesus, Lark. You know how much that night fucked me up. I can only imagine what you've had to deal with, carrying that secret all these years. Did you even go to therapy?"

Even though he wasn't looking at me, I could see his eyes turn glassy again, welling with a fresh wave of tears. "I didn't want to lie to you, but I was scared to tell you the truth. I don't know how, but I'll spend the rest of my life making it up to you. I promise."

"There's no need."

"Yes, there is. I swore I'd keep you safe and now I'm swearing to do whatever I have to to make you happy. Be whatever you need. Do whatever you want. I don't care. I don't care what people say. I just want to be worthy of you."

I took his face between my hands and forced him to meet my gaze. "You are. Please stop thinking you're not good enough. You're not *him,* if that's what you're worried about. And you never will be. You're ten times the man he ever was. You protect people, Larkin. And one day you'll protect people from other evil assholes like him. If that's the one good thing that comes from this, then that's enough. You were born to be a sheepdog. It's one of the many, *many* things I love about you."

"You know, you're the only one who ever really believed in me? Even when we were kids. Teachers were so fed up with me, with how far behind I was. Grandma kept the fucking knives locked up the first year I was there." A sad smile tipped the corner of his mouth. "But you? You insisted we play 'school' every day when we got home. And then you gave me a chocolate chip for every question I got right on our homework."

"I can't believe you remember that." I tried to fight a smile, but it came out anyway.

"I remember everything when it comes to you."

"Then you should know that I'll always believe in you. Just like I'll always love you. No matter where life takes us."

Larkin kissed me again with a renewed sense of urgency, as if that kiss was sealing an unspoken promise of sorts. This time, I didn't stop him. I returned each kiss with matching fervor, running my hands along his body and moaning when our hard-ons returned to full force, sliding against one another with each roll of our hips.

"I want you so fucking bad," Larkin panted against my lips. "I need to feel you, at least once. Please, Jame."

"It's not that I don't want to... It's just—I've never done it before," I admitted quietly, averting my gaze. The fact he wasn't a virgin when it came to intercourse and I was made my stomach churn. It was the one milestone we hadn't achieved at, or near, the same time. Seven years later and I'd yet to catch up.

"We'll figure it out together. Like always."

Glancing up at him, I was relieved to see a soft smile on his face instead of revulsion or annoyance. Punching your V card was still a big deal, at least for me, but after seeing the adoration in his eyes, I don't know why I'd even worried. "There's lube in the bottom drawer."

His smile turned wicked and he moved to retrieve it from the nightstand. A second after he opened the drawer, it dawned on me what *else* was in there. By the time Larkin rocked back on his heels, holding both the lube and my dildo, I was fairly certain I was beet red.

"Jesus, Kincaid. I don't know how I'm supposed to compete with this."

I glared at him. "It's not *that* big. And have you seen the size of your dick? Pretty sure you're thicker."

"I don't know," he murmured, holding the dildo alongside his own cock. "Guess we'll have to try them both out."

My eyes doubled in size. "What?"

"You heard me." He grinned, drizzling lube over the end of the dildo. "On your side."

Part of me wanted to protest out of sheer embarrassment, but the other, more dominant, part of me had me rolling onto my side in no time flat. Besides, if Larkin and I were going to go all the way, stretching things out beforehand was probably a good idea.

Adding some lube to my hole, Larkin pushed it in slowly with his finger, sending an array of sensations through me. The cold, slippery lube; his warm finger; the swirling pressure each time he pulled out, rubbing around the rim and stretching it gently.

"This is so much better than the couch," he said, sinking his middle finger inside and twisting slowly.

I moaned something along the lines of "Uh huh" and closed my eyes before they rolled into the back of my head and got stuck.

One finger became two. In and out, scissoring and swirling. And so much lube, I was afraid we were going to run out before we got to the main attraction.

Just when I'd gotten used to the rhythm of his fingers, a larger sensation pushed against my hole. Harder and colder than his fingers. The dildo. Taking note of its familiar mushroom head, the way it pushed into me without yielding, I exhaled and forced my body to relax by reminding myself this was everything I'd always wanted. A moment later, the dildo slipped inside, stretching me all around in ways that his fingers hadn't.

"Oh, fuck that's hot," Larkin whispered, caressing my ass with one hand while pushing the dildo deeper inside.

I gripped my asscheek and spread it wider, giving him more room to work with the toy. "You like that?"

He nodded, sliding the dildo in and out slowly, his eyes locked on my ass. "Hell yes. Wishing we'd done this sooner."

I couldn't agree more. Fucking myself with a dildo was one thing, but having someone else do it? And that someone being *Larkin*, of all people, made me want to pinch myself.

Even if this never happened again, at least I'd have this memory.

"Tell me how you want it," Larkin said, twisting the silicon cock inside until I moaned, clutching the sheets.

"Unpredictable," I panted, forcing myself to open my eyes and look over my shoulder at him. "I trust you."

He gave me another one of his wolfish grins, complete with dimples, and slid the dildo out, only to drive it in again. I cried out, more from surprise than anything, and glanced back to see he was watching me intently, varying the speed and depth that the toy plunged in and out.

On one particularly deep thrust, my eyes rolled up in my head and Larkin was on top of me again, kissing me with a raw hunger. I kissed him back, even as I reached down and withdrew the dildo. Tossing it to the side, I gripped his cock instead and guided it toward my hole.

"Are you sure?" he asked, his brows drawn together.

"Positive." I didn't want anything between Larkin and I —not secrets and not latex. Even though I was painfully aware of the fact I was still withholding one giant ghostly secret, I vowed to tell him at some point... just not tonight.

We locked eyes, each seeming to hold our breath as his freshly-lubed cock slid inside of me, demolishing what was left of my so-called boundaries and catapulting our friendship to a level we couldn't come back from.

Inch by inch, he pushed deeper. His dark lashes fluttered as he bottomed out and I swear to God I saw stars. I was so full, I was afraid to take a deep breath, let alone move.

"You feel fucking incredible," he breathed against my lips right before he kissed me. He didn't move either. We just stayed like that, kissing and caressing each other, while I got used to the feeling of his cock inside me. It was so different from the dildo I was used to but a thousand times better than I could have imagined.

Slowly, I rocked my hips back against his pelvis, tentatively fucking myself on his cock. He let me go for a bit, waiting until I'd picked up the pace, before he thrust into me.

"Oh my God," I breathed, reveling in the way sparks of pleasure shot throughout my body.

"Is this ok?"

"More than ok."

Just like with the dildo, he worked his way up gradually, varying the speed and how far his thrusts went. He'd let me get used to one way and then change it up on me, teasing me in the best of ways until he was pounding me mercilessly.

I was seconds away from coming when he rolled me onto my back and hooked one leg over his shoulder, thrusting steadily as he played with my cock.

"You're going to make me come like this," I said, swatting his hand away from my dick to try and buy myself some more time.

"Good." He slid my leg off his shoulder and leaned down, kissing me as deeply as he was fucking me.

When the panting got to be too much for our kisses, he gripped me by the back of the neck and pressed his forehead to mine, his eyes squeezed shut. It looked like he was fighting his own orgasm. If I had to guess, he was probably trying to hold off until I came.

"Fuck me harder," I groaned, stroking my cock as he did just that. "I want you to fill me up."

"Fuck..." He gritted his teeth and slid his other hand behind my neck, holding me in place as he thrust deep inside, again and again.

It didn't take long for the waves of pleasure to build in my balls before finally exploding in white bursts along my abs.

I clenched around him as my orgasm tore through me and Larkin gave a strangled cry before his hips slammed into me one last time, his cock pulsing inside. Sweaty though we were, he pressed his forehead to mine and his breath came in soft exhales across my skin.

"Now that was hot," I said, like a blissed-out moron.

He laughed and pulled back so he could look at me, though my legs were wrapped around his waist, keeping him and the mess inside. "You know I love you, right?"

"Yeah, I know that."

"No, I mean I *love* you, Jamie. Like, I'm *in* love with you, too. I just couldn't see it before. Or maybe I did and I didn't want to admit it."

"So what changed?" I traced my finger along the crease between his eyebrows. I didn't want to doubt him, and I sure as shit didn't want to ruin this moment, but I couldn't shake the feeling there was still something he wasn't telling me.

"Nothing. And everything. I guess the thought of losing you scared me. But also realizing I'd do anything for you. I mean, anything. Good or bad. And I've always felt that way. I thought that's what friends were supposed to do, but you're so much more than that. You've always been so much more than that."

"You're an idiot," I said with a smile. "And apparently a sappy idiot."

He scoffed and made a face at me. "You're sappy too. You still have this thing, for Christ's sake." He reached past me and unearthed Mr. Goose from beneath the pillow I was laying on. "I'm surprised it's held up as long as it has."

"Be careful with him!" I reached for the stuffed goose but Larkin sat up with it quickly, inspecting one of the wings. The fuzziness had worn off over the years from me holding it in that one spot, rubbing the plush material until I fell asleep.

"Why do you still have this thing?" he asked, genuine curiosity beneath the humor in his eyes.

"Because it's yours," I answered simply. "And apparently I *am* a sappy idiot, ok?"

"Told you." He smirked.

"Yeah, yeah." I took Mr. Goose from him gently and set him on the pillow, away from any lube or remnants of cum. "Where did you get him from, anyway? You never told me."

The light dimmed in his eyes. While he didn't look away, it did take him a moment to answer. "The cop who found me. He had it in his squad and gave it to me, told me it would keep me safe. Apparently geese are mean as shit, so he said it would chase the monsters away."

"Geese are mean? I had *no* idea," I said as sarcastically as I could, pressing my thumb against the dark bruise on his wrist.

"Ow! Jesus! Yes!" He yanked his hand away with a laugh, rubbing the goose bite gingerly. "And apparently they don't like being tackled while they're sleeping."

"Can't imagine why." I chuckled and slid off the bed, patting his knee. "We should probably get in the shower. And we definitely need a new blanket in here."

"We're not going to go again?"

I blinked at him, pausing in mid-step. "What?"

"I don't have much of a refractory period." He raked his teeth over his lower lip and scooted closer, drawing the tip of one finger along my shaft and making me shiver. "Doesn't look like you do either."

"Trying to make up for lost time?"

"Something like that."

"Mhmm. Well, unless you're going to try bottoming, stud, my ass has a refractory period, especially after all that."

"Ok." He didn't even blink. I did, though. Repeatedly.

"Ok? What do you mean 'ok'?"

"Ok, I'll bottom. I've never done it but you made it look good, so let's give it a whirl."

"A half hour ago you were straight. Now you want to bottom?"

"A half hour ago I was pretending to be someone else because I thought that's what I needed to do to get through life. Now, I don't care about that. All I care about is you. About us. And if you want to top, I'll bottom. If you want to bottom, I'll top. If you say you never want to have sex again, I'll cry, but I'll deal with it. I'll do whatever you want me to, just as long as you're with me."

"I appreciate that," I replied with a chuckle, running my hands through his hair.

He snagged me around the waist and pulled me into his lap, kissing my neck, seriousness edging out his earlier playfulness. "I just want you to be happy."

"That's all I've ever wanted for you too."

"I'm happy when I'm with you."

"Then it looks like we're stuck with each other."

"Nowhere I'd rather be." His dimples flashed and I pressed my lips to his, trying to pour all of my love and happiness into that kiss so maybe he'd feel a fraction of what I felt, what I'd *always* felt when it came to him. Larkin Galvan, my best friend and the absolute love of my life.

Chapter 7

Larkin

For the first time in forever, I was happy. Beyond happy. Elated. No—*in love.* Openly and with zero regard for what anyone had to say about it. I didn't give a fuck what anyone thought about me or who I chose to spend my life with. My only regret was waiting so long to embrace that mentality and inadvertently hurting Jamie along the way.

But all of that was water under the bridge. We had a new lease on life together and I was bound and determined to make the most of it.

Part of that, as much as I hated revisiting the past, was trying to get closure for the other families of the monster's victims.

Even though *he* was dead, dismembered, and scattered in the mountains of New Hampshire, I still needed to find his cache of photos. Most of all, I needed that fucking map. People needed bodies to get closure. Families wanted to lay their sons to rest. They were dead because of me and now I was their only hope of finding peace. How fucking twisted was that?

Still, it was something in my bones I knew I had to do. In a roundabout way, it was my way of making it up to Jamie, by doing right by all the others who came before him, the ones I *couldn't* save.

I'd combed through Sunderland looking for that damned truck, up every alley and backstreet, along the dirt roads on the outskirts. I even checked the tow yards and the police's impound lot. Nothing. No sign of the beat-up brown truck that had been lurking outside Grandma's house a week after her funeral. While I hadn't seen him in the truck, specifically, I knew his MO. He always went for older trucks that he could buy with cash because it meant no GPS tracking and an easy way to transport victims. It *had* to have been him, scoping out the place before he reared his ugly head.

The monster caught me off guard a month later when I was in the middle of packing up Grandma's things. Between classes and dealing with lawyers, I hadn't really put much thought into her house or the stuff inside. Once it was officially mine, I figured I better get my ass in gear before winter set in and the roads would be too shitty to make the trip up to Sunderland from Tennebrose.

I'd left the front door open so Jamie and I could haul boxes in and out easier. I still thanked God that Jamie had already left with a carful of donations when the monster crawled out of the past and back into my life. Except he probably knew that. Knowing him, he'd been watching us from the shadows, waiting for the right moment to strike.

A hunting knife dug into the side of my neck from behind a second before the stench of tobacco and cheap bar soap enveloped me.

"If you scream like a bitch, it'll be the last thing you do," he growled in my ear.

I froze in place, heart beating wildly against my ribs. *He found me.* I knew it without even looking. It had been years, but his voice was the same, brimming with a vile hatred that haunted my nightmares. "What the fuck are you doing here?"

"Is that any way to talk to your old man?" He snorted and the pressure on the knife shifted, sliding around my neck but not slicing as he moved in front of me. "See you're all grown up now."

"What do you want?" I said through my teeth.

"Figured now that meddling bitch is dead, you'd come on the road with me again. Pick up where we left off."

All I could do was stare at him, clenching my teeth even tighter before my mouth dropped open like a fish. There was no question he was evil as fuck, so I guess I was trying to decide if he was joking or if his insanity had reached new levels during our time apart.

"Don't you remember all the fun we had, kid? Don't you want that again?" Insane. He was truly fucking insane.

"I don't want anything to do with you," I replied as clearly as I could so he couldn't misconstrue my words. "The second you leave, I'm calling the cops. You deserve to rot for everything you did, you sick fuck."

His mouth twisted into a sneer beneath his dark beard. "Aw, don't do that. See if you do that, then I'm going to take your favorite toy away before I skip town. What's his name? Jamie? Yeah. You two seem real close."

A wave of dread crashed over me like ice water. He recognized Jamie. After all this time, he still fucking recognized him! Jamie's greatest fear was that he'd come back and now here he was, threatening my best friend's life once again.

A smile broke across the monster's face. "Yeah, I figured

that'd get your attention. Don't tell me you turned out to be a fag after everything I taught you? You know how fucking disgusting they are. How unnatural."

I didn't trust myself to answer, so I ground my molars together until my jaw ached.

"What do you think? Should we surprise him when he gets back? Let him see what a good time is all about? I'm sure you didn't get a lot of practice around this place, so I'll tell you what—I'll hold him for you and you can do whatever you want with him. Knives, fire, acid. Hell, I'll even let you fuck him one last time." His dark eyes lit up. "Your first one should be special. It's the most memorable, after all."

Rage replaced any sense of fear. My vision tunneled until a veil of black washed over everything.

I didn't remember reacting or even making a conscious decision *to* react. One minute the monster was standing there, a knife at my throat and that gut-wrenching smile on his face, and the next he was doubled-over, holding his hands over his face as blood gushed between his fingers. A dull pain registered in my forehead but it was nothing compared to the pounding in my temples as blood and adrenaline surged through me.

Snatching the knife off the floor, I jabbed it in his kidney and grabbed a fistful of his shirt, steering him toward the basement.

"You broke my fucking nose!" he hollered, unconcerned about the fact he was effectively my captive now.

"Shut the fuck up!" I pushed the knife in harder, surprised at how little resistance there was as the tip cut through the shirt and slid into his flesh. "Get down there," I snapped, shoving him down the basement stairs. I had to act fast. Sunderland wasn't that big and Jamie would be back at any second.

Bleeding from his nose and his side, the monster staggered through the basement. "Now what?"

"Sit over there." I directed him to one of the support posts.

As soon as he flopped onto the concrete floor, I took a tentative step away from him, scanning the immediate area for something to tie him up with. I found a combination of rope and bungee cords in a bucket, leftover from some gardening project Grandma had started in the spring and never finished because of her chemo treatments.

I secured his wrists to the post when the floorboards overhead squeaked.

"Lark?" Jamie yelled up above. "I'm back. They gave me some tax donation receipt thing. I don't know if you need it or not."

The knife flew to the monster's throat so fast, he flinched away from it, glaring up at me.

"Don't even fucking think about it," I whispered before yelling up to Jamie, "I'll be right there."

Returning his glare, I nudged his throat with the tip of the blade, a silent reminder to keep his trap shut while I grabbed a roll of duct tape. Slapping it over his mouth, I shoved the knife into my waistband and headed up the stairs, meeting Jamie with a forced smile. "Thanks for dropping that off."

"No problem." He gave me a brilliant smile and got back to work packing up a curio cabinet.

We loaded another carful of boxes and called it quits after I claimed I had a sociology paper to write. He never knew what ugly secret was hiding in the basement that day and God willing I'd never tell him.

I spent the next two days pacing my room and downing whatever alcohol I could get my hands on, alternatively trying to clear my head and forget everything that happened. After trying to forget *him*, forget my past, it came rushing back in fragmented pieces, ripping holes in my mind like shards of broken glass.

On the second night of his captivity, I drove back to Grandma's house. In my time away, he'd gotten out of my shitty restraints and ambushed me as soon as my feet hit the basement floor. We wrestled over the knife, ending in me slicing my hand open while somehow getting it away from him. I managed to get him tied up again, this time without the bungee cords, and I beat a hasty retreat back to Tennebrose, finishing a bottle of tequila along the way that did nothing to calm my nerves.

All I could think about was Jamie. He could never know what happened, how close he'd been to the man who tried to kill him. He'd finally gotten a handle on his anxiety, but with Halloween coming, I didn't need to stir up any more problems for him.

As soon as I saw the geese I had what I thought was a brilliant albeit drunken solution.

Farmers used guard geese to protect smaller flocks. I could get Jamie a goose. It would keep him safe, at least until I dealt with the monster, then the goose could take a hike and I'd be there to protect what was mine. A sheepdog fending off the wolves.

Parking my SUV, I crept up to the flock as they lay on the banks of one of Tennebrose's landscaped ponds, unaware of how vital they were to my best friend's safety.

My wrestling match with the goose went as well as it did with the monster. The bastard really did bite me, repeatedly, before flying away, leaving me in a heap on the cold ground.

Thanks to my efforts, my hand started bleeding like a

son of a bitch again, so I made my way to Jamie's residence hall with every intention of providing the security measures the runaway goose could not.

Now that the monster was dead and gone and I didn't need to worry about Jamie's safety, I could focus on finding that fucking truck and the trophies inside.

But it was gone.

I had no idea where else to look and without any sense of direction, I turned my own car around and headed back to Tennebrose—to Jamie. Halloween was closing in on us and I was on high alert when it came to his mood. He seemed to be doing ok, overall, but now that he knew the truth about the stranger who tried to murder him, I didn't want to take any chances of him having a panic attack or something.

As much as I may have wanted to give the other families closure, at the end of the day, Jamie was the only thing that truly mattered.

Chapter 8

Jamie

A week had passed since Larkin finally confessed his childhood horror and in that time he'd more or less moved in with me, without discussion. I mean, we already spent a lot of time together, but from that night on he made a point to sleep at my place *every* night. Not that I was complaining.

It was everything I'd ever wanted. I just wished it didn't come with such a horrible string attached. On the one hand, I felt some form of relief, knowing the stranger wasn't a stranger at all, that I didn't have to side-eye everyone who approached me too quickly or looked at me too long, wondering if they were going to strangle me out of nowhere. I didn't have to wonder who *he* was. I knew now—he was Larkin's father—and I wished I *didn't* know all at the same time. Because now I was side-eyeing my best friend, wondering if whatever evil was inside *him* had wound up inside his son.

But then Larkin would smile, dimples on full display, and I'd convince myself there was absolutely no way Larkin was anything like his barbaric father, that the first ten years of his life hadn't impacted him in any way beyond giving him equally, if not more, horrific nightmares than me and a desire to protect people from those who would take advantage of them. A true sheepdog.

And then I'd remember Cody's crumpled, broken face. The blood on Larkin's hands. Blood, I reminded myself, I'd cleaned off on more than one occasion when his anger got out of control. Is that how it started? Explosive rage? Beating someone to a pulp until there was nothing left to beat? What did one of his roommates say after he left Cody for dead in his room? *Larkin's a fucking psycho.*

When they weren't balled into fists, Larkin's hands were so gentle it was hard to imagine him hurting anyone, even if it meant protecting someone else. When they caressed my face or pulled me close, I trusted them implicitly. I played with them while we curled up with one another in bed, spoon-style, tracing along each of his fingers, following the pink line where I'd sutured his palm not too long ago. He was drunk when he cut it, claiming he was trying to capture a goose. Maybe he cut it on broken glass in the park. Maybe he ripped it open on a chainlink fence. There were a dozen possible scenarios, but none of them explained the cleanness of the cut. The only thing that did fit, however, was some sort of sharp-edged blade, like the kind you'd use to cut up a corpse, just like his father did...

Larkin wrapped his arms around me and squeezed tighter, kissing the back of my neck, derailing my train of thought before it went somewhere I couldn't come back from.

"Are we going to your grandma's house this weekend?" I asked in the quiet darkness of my bedroom.

"I suppose we should. I have to finish cleaning that stuff out before a realtor can come in."

"You don't want to keep it?"

"Fuck no." He held me closer, his breath warm against my skin as he buried his nose in my hair. "I'll get a place here in Winslow."

"You're still giving up on the FBI?"

"You're more important. Besides, if I get a few years under my belt on patrol, I have an even greater chance of getting in if you ever feel like relocating."

"Are you worried you won't?"

He got quiet for a moment. I could actually count the long pauses between each breath. Four in, hold, four out, hold; like he was trying to control his breathing. Or maybe he was on the verge of falling asleep.

"Because of your... past?" I ventured quietly, opting not to bring *him* into it directly. Still, I wished I could see Larkin's face, to see if he was worried or angry or sad. Maybe even relieved he didn't have to hide that part of his life anymore, that he could finally talk about it with someone, even if that someone was me, Victim Number I-Don't-Want-To-Know.

"They're going to know he was a killer," he replied just as quietly. "They're going to get those police reports. Those pictures..."

I rolled over to face him, linking my leg through his and caressing his cheek. It was hard to see much of his face with only a sliver of moonlight coming in through the cracks in the curtains. "That was all out of your control. You were a kid. They're going to know that."

"I didn't stop him."

"You *couldn't* stop him."

"I could have tried. I should have tried."

"He would have killed you too."

"Maybe he should have."

"Don't say that."

"If he had, he would have never had a reason to come back to New Hampshire. He would have stayed on the other side of the country and you would have been safe."

"But then I would have never known you."

"I'm sure you would've been just fine. You would have gone to Boston College and then conquered the world. Married rich. Adopted a brood of children. The family would go sailing on the weekends and use seasons like verbs." His voice shifted into an English accent. "Yes, Harold and I summered at the Cape with the children. It was brilliant. Are we wintering in the Caribbean this year, Schmoopy, or would you prefer Baja?"

I grinned at him, even as I shook my head. "Schmoopy? Really?"

His cheek twitched beneath my hand and I could hear the smile in his voice. "Snookums?"

"I'm not calling you Snookums."

"Well, no, 'cuz I'm not rich like Harold."

"I don't want Harold. I never wanted Harold. I only want you."

He leaned forward and pressed his lips to mine. It was tender for a moment before it turned fierce, possessive. I rolled my hips upward, deliberately rubbing my semi-hard cock against his through the thin material of our boxers. It was all the encouragement he needed before he was just as hard as I was.

Tearing his mouth from mine, Larkin shed his boxers before ripping mine off as well. As soon as we were both naked, he pounced, resuming his hungry kiss and grinding his dick against mine. He thrust down as I thrust up, our tongues and cocks slipping and sliding against each other.

With our bodies pressed together, we had plenty of friction, but apparently Larkin wanted more.

He spat into his palm and reached between us, stroking both of us at the same time. Moaning into his mouth, I twined my arms around his neck and plunged my tongue deeper, caressing his with mine. I thrust up into his hand and rolled my hips, changing the pressure and the angle of how our cocks rubbed against each other.

"Fuck, Jame," Larkin breathed, releasing his hold so he could brace himself above me with both arms, alleviating some of his weight. He might have thought he was crushing me, but I wanted it. I wanted to feel him against me.

"You gonna come?" I slid my hands down his back and grabbed his ass, squeezing it and pulling him closer.

He nodded frantically and dropped to his elbows, slanting his mouth over mine.

We rocked against each other, faster and faster, thrusting and swiveling, until our bodies were covered in a sheen of sweat beneath the heavy comforter. Each breath grew more and more ragged and our kisses turned sloppy in desperation.

As much as I wanted him to come first for a change, I couldn't help the swell building inside of me, nor could I stop it once it finally unleashed, jetting all over my abs.

Swiping a handful of cum off my stomach, I gripped Larkin's cock and jacked him with the makeshift lube, hard and fast the way he preferred to finish.

He seized my face in both hands and kissed me hotly, fucking my mouth with his tongue as he fucked himself in my fist. It wasn't long before the first spurt of cum shot across my hand, smearing across my stomach and mixing with what was already there.

Pressing his forehead against mine, Larkin closed his eyes and swallowed hard, trying to catch his breath.

"I love you," I whispered, brushing my nose against his.

"I love you more." His eyes opened as he spoke and he gave me one of his heart-stopping smiles.

Deep down, I knew he was nothing like his father and I admonished myself for ever doubting him.

A silvery glow bled through my eyelids, slicing into my peaceful haze of sleep.

"Dude, turn your brightness down," I grumbled, squeezing my eyes tighter while swatting blindly at Larkin and his cell phone.

He didn't answer or even grunt an apology.

"Why are you awake, anyway?" I scrunched my pillow under my head and settled down again, but the brightness behind my closed eyes hadn't diminished. "Are you ok?"

Still, no answer.

I opened my eyes only to see Larkin was fast asleep, one arm tucked under his head and the other stretched toward me. Neither held his cell phone. A quick glance confirmed it was still charging on the nightstand behind him.

A cold sweat broke out along the back of my neck.

The silvery glow shifted in my periphery, at the foot of the bed.

My heart hammered. Blood rushed to my head, making it hard to hear anything above the spastic whooshing and thumping in my ears.

The heavy feeling of an unseen gaze crushed me and that damn glow could have only meant one thing.

It was a ghost.

Did I turn and face it? Did I wake Larkin? There had been a few times I'd encountered a ghost around him, but never at home, never while I was fucking asleep! Since the dorms were part of university housing, the facilities and grounds crew kept the buildings warded. So how did it get in here?

"Mortem obire," I whispered out loud.

The glow didn't abate.

Turning my head slowly, I clutched the comforter and steeled myself.

It was *him*. The stranger. There was no mistaking the ugly scar that ran down the side of his face or the scraggly dark beard that did a poor job of hiding it. Except, he wasn't a stranger anymore. I knew who he was, though it was little comfort with him a mere four feet away from me.

Standing in the sliver of moonlight, he glared at me, his face as monstrous as it was *that* night.

Was he alive? Is that why Dr. Corbin's phrase didn't work? Was he moments away from finishing me off while his son slept peacefully next to me?

Before I could summon the courage to try the words again, he lunged at me.

I screamed and threw myself to the side, out of bed, away from Larkin. The comforter tangled around my foot, sending me crashing into the corner where my dresser met the wall.

Larkin shouted my name.

Someone grabbed my arms from behind, spinning me around. I thrashed wildly. Larkin repeated my name, over and over, but it took a moment to realize it was him trying to help me up, not his father trying to kill me again.

"It's me," Larkin said, touching my cheek gently. "You're ok."

"He was here!" I screamed, looking past him frantically. "He was just here!"

"Who was here?"

"Him! *Him*! Your—the stranger!"

Larkin's shoulders rounded as he let out a breath, something between a sigh of relief and an irritated exhalation. "That's not possible, Jame."

"I swear to God, he was here."

He fixed me with a calm, patient look, but one that said, quietly, "I don't believe you." Taking my hand in his, he gave it a gentle squeeze.

Tears pricked my eyes and my throat started to close. Throwing my arms around him, I heaved a new wave of panicked breaths against his bare shoulder. With the anniversary of my near-death on the horizon and Larkin's confession still ringing in my ears, maybe I *was* seeing things, or dreaming them. Maybe this was my subconscious's way of dealing with it all.

Stroking my hair, Larkin whispered the same calming placations he'd used for almost a decade. As always, he sounded so certain everything would be ok, that I would be safe and he would make sure nothing happened.

Except, this time was different. This time my so-called gift had clashed with the trauma that brought it about in the first place and I couldn't sort the supernatural from the psychotic. I knew what that silver glow meant because I'd been seeing it ever since that monster dragged me to the edge of death and Larkin pulled me back. But I also knew that face, that scar, and the fact the magic ghost words didn't work on him.

"I *know* I saw him," I whispered once my breathing slowed down. "He was here, Larkin. In the room."

"That's not possible," Larkin repeated, a little slower, a little firmer than before. It wasn't disbelief that fueled his words, it was absolute certainty.

"Why? What didn't you tell me?"

"He's dead, Jamie. He can't hurt you anymore."

"How do you know he's dead?" When Larkin didn't answer right away, a shiver ran down my spine. I pulled back, eyes wide. "Oh my God... what did you do?"

"What?" Larkin frowned at me. "What are you—"

"Don't. Do not come up with some bullshit to feed me right now. How did you get that cut on your hand? That wasn't all your blood. It couldn't have been."

"I didn't kill him," Larkin said quickly.

"Then who did?"

Larkin laughed and gave a helpless shrug. "I don't know. God? Maybe it was a heart attack. Maybe he ruptured something the last time we fought, when he tried to gut me with a knife. All I know is that when I went back to my grandma's house—"

"He was at your grandmother's house?!"

"—he was dead."

"What the fuck was he doing at your grandmother's house?!"

"Fucking with me."

"So the night I saw him on campus, that was really him. I told you! I fucking told you I saw him!"

"No." Larkin shook his head vehemently. "He was chained in the basement. It couldn't have been him."

"You chained him in the basement?! Jesus Christ!" I

pushed away from him, only managing a few wobbly steps as I kicked away the bedding tangled around my ankles.

Larkin was right behind me, his hand on my arm, pulling me back. "He threatened you, Jamie! There was no way I was going to let him get within twenty feet of you."

"So you chained him in the fucking basement?!" I whirled on him, pushing his hand off my bicep. "What was the plan? Why didn't you call the police?"

"I was going to! I wanted to find enough evidence to put him away first. I couldn't let him get away a second time."

"And the police were totally cool with the fact you were holding him prisoner when he mysteriously died?"

His jaw shifted and mine dropped.

I covered my mouth with my hands, gaping at him. When I finally lowered them in preparation to speak, he looked away.

"Larkin, what did you do?" I whispered. It was my turn to do the lunging. I grabbed his biceps and squeezed, trying to get him to look at me. "Tell me you called the police. Tell me you—"

"Cut him up into little pieces and threw the remains along the mountain. I burned and bleached away the rest of the evidence. He's *gone*, Jamie. He's fucking gone. And the world is better off for it." He exhaled a slow breath and took my hands in his, squeezing gently. "I'm sorry I didn't tell you. I understand if you can't look at me the same way after hearing that. Just know that I did it to keep you safe. And you are. Finally. But that also means there's no way he was here tonight. You're free, Jame. He can't hurt you anymore."

Unable to speak, I simply nodded.

There's no way I could tell him *my* secret now. Larkin's ghost-free life would never mesh with my... not so ghost-free life, no matter how much I might have wanted it to. He knew all my fears, all my secrets—except one. *This* one.

In Larkin's world, humans were worse than any ghost could ever be. It was one thing to be the son of a killer, to have endured the childhood Larkin had. Even disposing of the body made sense, given the circumstances of who had died and where. I couldn't blame him for not wanting to involve the police.

But to tell someone who had witnessed evil firsthand that you see ghosts? Yeah, no. Larkin had enough guilt from that night because of what his father did to me. There was no way I could burden him with the whole ghost bit on top of everything else. He'd already suffered in silence for so long, trying to protect my feelings and keep me from losing my mind. It was my turn to protect him from this.

Chapter 9

Jamie

As a kid, the countdown to Halloween felt like it took forever until one glorious October morning, it arrived. Sometimes with sun, sometimes pouring down rain. A few times it even snowed. No matter what the weather was like, nothing could stifle the excitement that buoyed me and all the other kids in Sunderland. It was *Halloween*. It was *our* holiday, one where we could be whatever we wanted and roam the neighborhood, making demands out of adults we'd otherwise never talk back to.

There was a magic to that day that only grew stronger with each carved jack-o-lantern set out on doorsteps and each hazy ghost hung from tree branches. Glittering orange and purple lights seemed to reflect a shimmer in the air, adding to the moonlit distortions and glowing pumpkins. It didn't matter what town in America you were in, the transcendental spirit of Halloween was everywhere. You couldn't escape it.

Sadly, even Tennebrose wasn't immune.

Like all the years before, the surrounding Winslow area

was transformed from an austere, Puritan university town to one of ancient mysteries and whimsical scares. And for every wart-faced witch and grinning skeleton I passed on my way to class, my anxiety ratcheted up to another level until I was jumping and gasping every two feet like a moron.

I tried reminding myself what Larkin told me—that his father, my would-be murderer, was dead, but it didn't do me any good. I still saw his ugly face everywhere I went. On campus, in the crowd. In store windows, next to paper ghosts and screeching black cats. In Halloween displays that took over people's yards like a series of tableaux vivants straight out of my nightmares.

Every time I saw it, I said the words Dr. Corbin gave me. *Mortem obire.* Over and over. It didn't matter, though. *He* was always there, watching me.

The final straw came one afternoon when I screamed the Latin words in front of witnesses like a lunatic. I watched the killer's ghostly face fade, slowly, on *his* terms, while the people milling about on the beautiful fall day merely saw me shouting at a happy-faced scarecrow listing in someone's front yard next to a bale of straw.

I bolted back to the dorms and hurled myself at my desk, tearing through the drawers to try and find the one scrap of paper that could help me.

Larkin found me up to my elbows in old papers and stacks of textbooks a short time later. "You ok?"

"Have you seen Dr. Corbin's business card?"

"Uh, no. Why? Do you need me to take you to the hospital?"

"No!" I shot him a glare and clawed through another desk drawer. "I need his number, not the hospital."

"Why?"

"Because I need it!" I snapped.

"Hey." Larkin's hands landed on my shoulders, holding me in place and giving me a gentle squeeze. "What's going on?"

I exhaled a calming breath and met Larkin's concerned gaze. "I need his help with something."

"But you won't tell me?"

"You wouldn't believe me," I said, pushing past him and heading to the fridge. Hopefully the card was stuck in the slew of takeout menus. If not, maybe I could plead with the hospital staff to page him for me or something.

"That's bullshit!" Larkin was right behind me, every step of the way. "You're not even giving me a chance! And after everything I told you?"

"I tried to tell you the other night! You didn't listen!"

"Tell me what? That you saw *him*? That he was in your room?" Larkin ran a hand over his face, lowering his voice when he spoke again. "That was a bad dream, Jame. That's all."

"No, it wasn't!" I slammed the handful of menus on the tiny kitchen table. "I told you I saw him before that, too! I've *been* seeing him! And it doesn't matter that he's dead because—" The truth stalled on my tongue, unwilling to come out.

"Because what?" He spread his hands, waiting.

This must have been how Larkin felt before he confessed his deepest, darkest secrets, teetering on the edge of hope and fear of rejection. Desperate to let it all out, to unburden himself, but paralyzed by a myriad of possible outcomes, most of which ended horribly.

"Jamie! Just fucking say it!"

I spit it out in a rush, like ripping off a bandaid again. "Because I can see ghosts."

Larkin blinked, a small crease forming between his dark brows.

"I know," I continued. "It's crazy. Ghosts aren't real. Except, they are. I've been seeing them since we were thirteen. Dr. Corbin said I'm a medium. I guess sometimes experiences like mine give you the ability. I swear to you, it's not all in my head. They're real."

"You never said anything," Larkin said quietly, looking more like a wounded puppy than someone trying to process the unbelievable.

"I told my parents when it first started. They told my shrink. They all said it was trauma and upped my medication, but I still saw them. I didn't understand any of it until our freshman year here when Dr. Corbin explained what was happening. Finally, everything made sense."

"Yeah... but you still never said anything to me." His dark eyes dropped for a moment as his mouth curved into a frown. "Even after you knew for sure it was real."

My gaze fell to the center of his chest, guilt seeping in to replace the relief ballooning inside. "I didn't want you blaming yourself any more than you already do for what happened back then. And before you told me what really happened, I didn't want to give you a reason to not like me or to think I was weird."

"Are you serious? After the shit I dropped on you? You think *I'm* going to judge you for talking to Casper?" He nudged me, prompting me to look up again. "Besides, you're already weird. Science nerd."

"So you believe me?" All ribbing aside, I couldn't help the lingering doubt. Other than Dr. Corbin, no one else had taken me seriously. They all wanted to "fix" me and make me "normal" again, but how were you supposed to do that after seeing how ugly the world can be?

"Of course I believe you. My great-aunt used to pass on messages from our dead relatives. I always thought it was kinda cool." He closed the distance between us and touched my face. Leaning in, he stopped abruptly and glanced around. "We're alone, though... right?"

I grinned and nodded. As his lips pressed against mine, the huge weight I'd been carrying for all those years drifted away from me, replaced by complete happiness. It was hard to remember what I'd been so afraid of. Larkin had never ridiculed me or made me feel bad about anything in all the years I'd known him. He'd always been by my side, no matter what, just like I would always stand by his.

Pulling away gently, Larkin frowned at me again. "But seriously, why do you need to talk to Dr. Corbin?"

"Because of *him*," I replied glumly. "I've been seeing him, like I said, and he's not leaving even though I've told him to a dozen times."

"You *told* him to?"

"Yeah. It's a Latin thing. It's supposed to make ghosts move on but it's not working with him."

"Probably because he has unfinished business. Isn't that why ghosts stick around?"

An involuntary chill crept down the back of my neck. "I don't even want to think about what that could be."

"Can you ask him?"

"I'd prefer not to. But I'm sure Dr. Corbin can."

Pulling up to the massive black iron gates, Larkin slowed his SUV to a stop and rolled down his window.

"How'd you know where he lives?" I asked. After being unable to locate the elusive doctor at the hospital or at Tennebrose, Larkin suggested we try his house. Even if Dr. Corbin wasn't home, we were hoping someone would be able to get me in contact with him. But until we were actually sitting in front of a stately residence in the middle of nowhere, I hadn't thought to ask how we were going to get his address.

"Did a ride along with Chief Treadwell at the beginning of the semester," Larkin replied. "It kind of stuck out on his tour of important places in Winslow."

"I can see why."

"I wonder if there's a call box or something?" The words had barely left his lips when the gates swung open. "I guess maybe there's a sensor? Or cameras?"

I shrugged.

Larkin maneuvered his SUV through the gates and headed down the long drive.

The Corbins' mansion looked like it belonged in a fairytale. Massive, old stones made up the construction, complete with turrets and diamond-shaped windows. Ivy covered one side of the building and there were balconies and chimneys galore. It was magnificent.

We'd just climbed the front steps, poised to bang one of the heavy iron rings on the intricately carved door when Dr. Corbin appeared from around the side of the house, a small brown and white goat frolicking beside him on the perfectly manicured lawn.

"I thought I heard a car," Dr. Corbin said with a smile. "What can I do for you?"

"It's about a ghost," I said, cutting right to the chase. When Dr. Corbin's gaze flicked to Larkin, I backtracked a bit with a wince. "He knows. I told him... about me. He won't say anything, I promise."

Larkin nodded in agreement.

"Ah. I see." Dr. Corbin glanced between us again. "Come in, then. Don't mind Kevin. He should be in the stable, but he has a fondness for the kitchen and it's almost impossible to keep him out." He opened the front door and gestured inside as the goat darted ahead of us.

We followed Dr. Corbin—and Kevin—to the kitchen and sat where directed.

"Tea? Coffee?" he asked politely, though the last thing my frazzled nerves needed was caffeine of any kind.

"No thank you," I replied.

"I'm good," Larkin added.

"Well, then. Straight to the matter at hand." Dr. Corbin slid into a seat across from us and folded his hands on the table. "What can I do for you?"

"Do you remember when you first told me about all of this ghost stuff my freshman year?" I asked, to which Dr. Corbin nodded. "There's a ghost that won't leave me alone. And '*mortem obire*' isn't working."

He frowned, rubbing one thumb over the knuckle of the other. "Tell me more about this spirit."

"Uh..." I stole a glance at Larkin, not sure how much I should actually say about this ghost in particular.

"Is it someone you know?" Dr. Corbin prompted.

"Kind of."

"An acquaintance with a fairly recent passing?"

"He's not an acquaintance... exactly..."

"He tried to murder Jamie when we were kids," Larkin said bluntly. His hand slid over my knee beneath the table, but his gaze was fixed on the professor.

"Oh." Dr. Corbin's eyes widened. "That does change things."

"What do you mean?" My heart plummeted.

"Normally spirits are neutral beings, even benevolent if they choose. But a murderer or similarly evil person is much more likely to continue to inflict damage in the afterlife. The fact this one has a personal link to you only makes it stronger."

"Is that why the words didn't work?"

"More than likely. You have to do more than bid the spirit adieu. You must banish it."

"How do we do that?" Larkin asked, ever the problem solver.

Dr. Corbin shrugged. "It depends. How gruesome do you want to get?"

"As gruesome as necessary," Larkin replied without hesitating.

"For the fast and surefire way, dig up the corpse and pour salt over it before setting it on fire. Then rebury the remains in consecrated ground. Churchyards are usually best, but it can be any land sprinkled with some holy water. There may or may not be a perfect spot in the back corner of the Old Burying Ground here in Winslow that's more or less shielded from the road, if someone had a vehicle with four-wheel drive." He looked pointedly at Larkin.

Larkin swallowed thickly and gave a curt nod while I gaped at Dr. Corbin before spitting out, "Is there a slightly *less* gruesome, not to mention illegal, option?"

Dr. Corbin considered it for a moment. "Halloween is almost here. I can write down a longer incantation to try, along with a cleansing ritual. That might be enough to solve your problem without doing anything drastic."

"And if it doesn't work?" Larkin asked as I slumped back in my chair, feeling less and less confident by the moment.

"I hope you know where the body is buried." Dr. Corbin smiled. Behind him, the goat bleated in agreement.

Chapter 10

Larkin

"Do you think he knows?" I asked after we were on the main road, headed back to Winslow, and far, far away from the huge, creepy house in the woods.

"Knows what?" Jamie asked, reading over Dr. Corbin's weird shopping list for the tenth time.

"About *him*? About what I did?"

"I doubt it. Even if he did, he's the one who told us to dig up a corpse, which I'm sure is very illegal, even in Winslow. Not to mention that whole cemetery thing."

"That's the other problem—there's nothing to dig up, remember? So if the magical weeds don't work, then what?"

"Then I guess we're taking a day trip back to Sunderland to look for some body parts."

"I couldn't ask you to do that."

"You're not asking me to do anything. We're in this together." Jamie gasped suddenly and braced against the dash with both hands. "Look out!"

My headlights flashed across something white in the roadway. I slammed on the brakes. The tires smoked and we skidded to a halt sideways in the road.

"What the fuck was that?" I asked, craning in my seat to check the dark pavement behind us. It was empty, except for a swirl of orange and brown leaves. "I don't see anything."

"It was him." Jamie exhaled and ran a hand over his face, looking like a ghost himself.

"Next time, let me run his ass over." I gradually pushed on the gas, resuming our drive, though I kept both hands on the wheel and a watchful eye on the rearview mirror, waiting for the sick bastard to pop out like the killer in a slasher film.

"I don't know what happens if they touch someone who can't see them. You might get hurt or possessed or something. The one time it happened to me, my arm was cold for over an hour."

"Is that what Dr. Corbin meant by 'inflicting damage'? I thought they just moved pictures and shit?" I snuck a glance at him out of the corner of my eye.

"Some do. Others can possess you. Even kill you, or get you to kill yourself, which is pretty much the same thing." Jamie turned to look out the window, but the paper in his hand crinkled as he clutched it a little tighter.

At a loss for words, I took his other hand and squeezed it gently. Here I'd been harboring secrets from him and I never once stopped to think he'd have secrets of his own.

I was glad he finally told me, though. So much about our past fell into place with that bit of information. His reactions on field trips to museums and historic houses, how he hated ghost decorations in particular, and why he was so jumpy in the dark. It wasn't *just* Halloween and the PTSD from surviving my father. It wasn't a lingering (and totally justified) paranoia that the monster would come back for him. No, it was so much more. My best friend was haunted, literally, by that night and he didn't even feel comfortable enough to tell me.

A pang of failure wormed through my chest, like it was nothing more than a piece of rotten fruit.

"So what's it like?" I asked quietly. If I was ever going to understand his ability, it seemed like I should start with the basics.

"Seeing ghosts?"

"Yeah."

"It's... weird. Some of them are really easy to tell because they'll have this glow. Or be transparent. Some are really disfigured, but others look normal."

"And what do you do when you see them?"

"I mutter in Latin." He chuckled quietly. "Nerd, I know. But, if the person disappears, they were a ghost. If they don't, then I get concerned for their Vitamin D intake."

"I thought those were medical terms you kept quizzing yourself on," I said with a half-grin, squeezing his hand.

He chuckled again, which is what I was hoping for. "Because that's what I told you it was. I guess I could have said it was a prayer or something."

"Yeah, except you're not Catholic."

"See, this is the problem with trying to hide things from you. You know too much about me." He said it jokingly, but my guts twisted regardless.

"I'm sorry I made you feel like you couldn't tell me the truth," I said quietly. "You shouldn't have had to go through that alone. Not after everything else."

He squeezed my hand. "It's ok. Really. I'm at peace with it now. I just didn't want to burden you any more than I already did. Do."

"You were *never* a burden, Jamie."

"Sure feels that way. Even now, dragging you into my ghost problems."

"I'll take your ghost problems over my daddy issues any day of the week."

A laugh bubbled out of him and he clamped a hand over his mouth, looking wide-eyed at me. "I'm sorry," he said, lowering his hand and trying to regain his composure. "I didn't mean to laugh."

"Mhmm. No, I see how it is." I sniffed and tipped my chin up theatrically. "I have one moment of vulnerability and it bites me in the ass. I'm so glad I can be your comic relief, Kincaid."

"I'll make it up to you *and* your ass." When I stole another glance at him, he leaned across the center console and licked my neck before biting it, sending a rush of goosebumps across my skin. "After we get the herbs," he added.

"Fuck the herbs." I shifted closer to him, trying to capture a kiss, but he shook his head and retreated to his side of the car.

"No way. Shopping first."

"Then sex."

"Then the incantation Dr. Corbin gave me."

"*Then* sex?"

"Then sex."

"Fuck yes." I gunned it for the flower shop in downtown Winslow. The sooner we could get what we needed, the sooner we could go home and do the ritual thingie and the sooner we'd both be to achieving orgasmic bliss.

Once we were loaded up with bundles of herbs and a potted plant from the flower shop and gobs of overpriced candles from the artisan candle store, not to mention the bag full of crystals Dr. Corbin shoved at Jamie before we left, we headed home.

Back in Jamie's dorm, he drew a bath and sprinkled a concoction of pink salt and dried leaves and petals into the water. To spiritually cleanse or detach or something. I wasn't really paying attention to Dr. Corbin's spiel earlier—I was too busy looking around the dungeon of doom that was his basement. That shit was straight out of *Macbeth*. Skulls on shelves. Jars of… stuff. Loads of crystals and candles and bowls. Books that looked like they should be in a museum somewhere.

It was all kind of surreal. Dr. Corbin was a *doctor* doctor, not just someone with advanced education. A well-known, highly respected surgeon. He was a man of hard science and facts and biology, like Jamie. And yet the two of them had been deeply engrossed in an intense conversation about when to use onyx and when to use jet, even though both of the black stones basically did the same thing.

They were taking the whole thing so seriously that it was hard to discount their belief in ghosts, even though I remained firmly in the "I have no fucking clue" camp. I didn't know if I believed in ghosts, but I believed in Jamie and if *he* believed, then I believed by proxy. The story about my great-aunt hadn't been a lie, either. When I first heard about it I thought it *was* cool, but the general consensus in the family was that her cheese had slid off her cracker and we were supposed to humor an old lady who missed her deceased relatives. In hindsight, maybe she was on to something.

Even if I was undecided on the matter of ghosts, I had a feeling the lady at the flower shop knew what was up. Before we walked out with our brown paper bag of herbs, she stopped me in my tracks and handed me a pot of lavender.

"To help you see," she said simply.

"Uh, thanks?" See what? I didn't ask, since she said it like I should know what the hell she was talking about.

When I reached for my wallet a second time, she waved me off and said, "Good luck." Not "Thanks for stopping in" or "Good night." I suppose I should have been more weirded out by it, but after four years of calling Winslow home, interactions like that didn't strike me as odd as they once did. People in this town seemed to say or do the most random things and no one really batted an eye. Maybe that's why Jamie wanted to stay here after he graduated—he found his people.

"Can I get you anything?" I asked Jamie as he sank into the bath water.

"Just you."

"I don't think we'll both fit," I said with a laugh, knowing for a fact the pitiful tub/shower combo wouldn't be relaxing for one, let alone two, of us.

"We can try."

I met his innocent smile with a grin. "Let me go get some of those magical candles we just bought. We can really set the mood."

"Sounds good."

I closed the bathroom door to keep the steam in and cut across to the kitchenette.

Water splashed behind the door.

"Did you forget something?" I asked, grabbing a couple of the candles and tucking them in the crook of one arm while I searched for a lighter in the junk drawer.

More water cascaded down the side of the tub, followed by a banging sound.

"Jamie?" I frowned at the noise—and the lack of response to my earlier question.

Setting the candles on the table, I hurried back to the bathroom and threw the door open.

Jamie's head was completely submerged. His arms, however, stuck straight up out of the water, like he was trying to push someone off. Or some*thing*. No matter how much he flailed around in the tub, he didn't resurface.

I didn't give a fuck about the risks of touching a ghost. Sprinting to the bathtub, I grabbed onto Jamie's shoulders and yanked him up as hard and as fast as I could. I expected some sort of supernatural resistance or something, but there was none. Jamie shot up out of the water like a rocket, coughing and sputtering and clawing wildly at the front of my shirt.

"You're ok," I said, hauling him out of the tub and wrapping him in a towel, rubbing his arms briskly as I steered him to the bedroom. "You're ok, Jamie. Just try to take a breath."

"He said he's going to kill me," Jamie said between coughs, clinging to the front of my shirt.

"I'm not going to let that happen. Do you hear me?" I hugged him fiercely, trying to stop the trembling in his body with my warmth and solid reassurance.

The only problem was... how was I supposed to protect him from someone who was already dead?

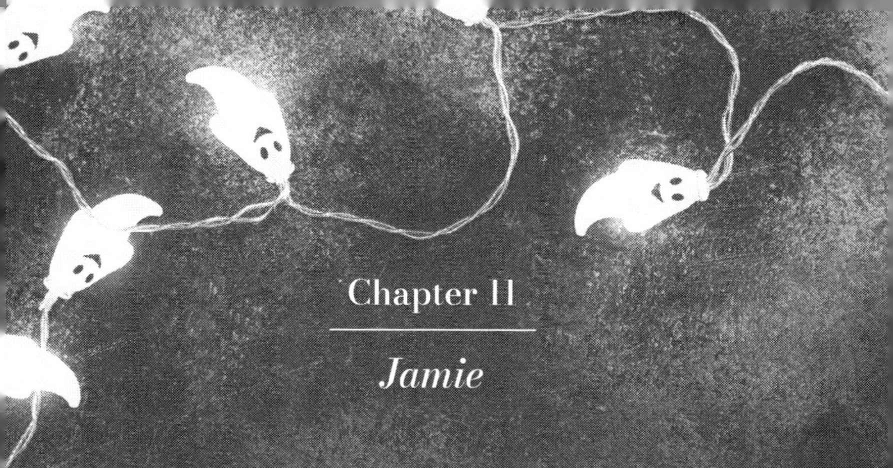

Chapter 11

Jamie

My Critical Theory class was almost over when Dr. Corbin stuck his head in and caught my eye. He and the other professor exchanged a nod before Dr. Corbin tipped his chin up at me in a silent beckon. I gathered my stuff and sheepishly headed out the door, ducking my head so I could avoid the curious stares of my classmates. Not that I wasn't grateful to miss the last ten minutes of a riveting lecture on the theoretical underpinnings of the American healthcare system, but it did feel a bit like being called to the principal's office.

"How are you?" Dr. Corbin asked, keeping his voice low in the hallway. "Did you do the bath?"

I nodded, hating that not only had I failed his ghostly extracurricular assignment but I almost drowned in the process like a total loser.

Dr. Corbin frowned. "What happened?"

"I..." I debated lying to him, but since I was the one who'd gone to him for help, I opted for the truth. Clearing my throat, I waited for another student to wander by before I finished answering. "It didn't work."

"Why not? What happened, exactly?"

"The ghost tried drowning me." I winced from both shame and the memory of that invisible pressure weighing down on me, the unbearable burning sensation as water filled my lungs, being unable to scream for help even though help was in the other room.

"Are you sure you're alright, then? Jamie, I'm so sorry. That ritual has never failed me before. I've done it myself—countless times."

"It's not your fault. I probably messed it up somehow."

"Impossible. Even with only half of the ingredients, the spell should have worked because the intention was there." His brow furrowed as he looked away, mulling everything over in silence. After a moment, he straightened, looking more optimistic than before. "Perhaps you're not the attachment."

"What do you mean?"

"If that ritual didn't work then maybe it's because *you* are not what this spirit is attached to. There has to be someone—or something—else keeping it here."

My thoughts went straight to Larkin. "So if the other person does the ritual, he'll go away?"

"Yes. So long as that other person is the anchor holding him here and it's not some obscure location. Otherwise, I suggest you go with the gruesome option. That will sever any tie that might remain."

"That's not really an option though. I don't know where the body is," I whispered, stealing a cautious glance around the hallway. "He wasn't exactly buried."

"Then hopefully the other bath works."

"And if it doesn't?"

He patted my shoulder with a gentle, fatherly sort of smile. "Believe that it will. Believe in the power of

Halloween. If the bath doesn't work today, tomorrow is the last chance, while the veil between realms is at its thinnest. Otherwise, you'll need to go on a scavenger hunt and do the gruesome ritual I know you'd rather avoid."

"Can't you help? Tell the ghost to go away, like you said you would?"

"It's a bit more complicated than that, I'm afraid."

"Why?"

"Because of the link it has to you and the other person. Even if I were to step in, there's no guarantee it wouldn't find its way back to you. If that happens, there's a chance it could come back as something even worse."

"What could be worse than the ghost of a serial killer?"

"A demon." He said it with such solemnity that all I could do was blink. Even though I knew about the existence of ghosts, I never considered the possibility of other *things* being out there in the world. I could barely handle ghosts leering at me, so I definitely didn't want to take my chances with a demon. "That's why it's important for you to be the one to handle it," Dr. Corbin continued. "To ensure it's gone for good. And in the process, you'll strengthen your abilities, which will serve you long after you've left Tennebrose."

"What if I'm not able to do it?"

"You will. Believe in yourself, Jamie. You have the magic of Halloween on your side. It's why this is a fortuitous time of year, not something to be feared."

I scoffed. "Halloween is what got me into this shit show in the first place."

"Do you know much about the history of Halloween?"

"Not really."

"Well, it wasn't always candy and pumpkins. It was the Celtic new year, a time for renewal. Despite entering the darkest half of the year, it wasn't doom and gloom for our ancient ancestors, it was part of life's cycle and they embraced it. It was a chance to reunite with relatives who had passed on and secure their blessing for the year ahead."

It didn't feel like the time for a fresh beginning, but I was inclined to take Dr. Corbin at his word. He hadn't steered me wrong so far, though I'd be lying if I said I wasn't disappointed he wouldn't swoop in and take care of the ghost himself.

Handing me a business card, Dr. Corbin gave me a reassuring smile. "Call me if the bath doesn't work on Larkin."

"I will." He was a few steps away when I spun, mouth agape. "I never said he was the other person!"

Dr. Corbin chuckled, never slowing his stride. "You didn't have to."

"You want me to take a bath in the same tub you nearly drowned in, doing the same thing that you were doing when you nearly drowned?" Larkin asked slowly, both eyebrows raised so high they were nearly in his hairline.

I nodded. "Yeah. You have to."

"Why?"

"Dr. Corbin said so."

"No offense to the good doctor, but his little ritual didn't work on you so why the hell would I do it?"

"Because you're the reason *he* is still around. Dr. Corbin thinks he's attached himself to you, not me. You have to separate yourself and then I can say the incantation to get rid of him for good."

Larkin sighed and got to his feet, peeling off his t-shirt. "Fine. Let's do this."

I recreated the same bath from the night before, only this time I stayed in the room with Larkin. There was no way on God's green earth I was leaving anything to chance.

After a couple awkward moments of silence, Larkin looked up at me from the tub and spread his hands. "Now what?"

"I don't know." Shrugging, I shifted on the edge of the tub, trying to find a way to get remotely comfortable on the narrow perch.

"Am I supposed to feel something?"

"I don't know," I sighed.

"K..."

"I guess we wait for *him* to show up."

"Well, that's all you, since I can't see shit."

"Didn't the lady at the flower shop give you something for that?"

"Yeah, it's in the kitchen."

"After this, I guess, put some in your pocket. Along with the piece of jet from Dr. Corbin."

"Yes, sir," he said with a faux salute.

"Smart ass," I shot back, splashing water in his face.

Laughing, he sliced his hand through the top of the water and more or less flung it at me, dousing my side.

"Larkin!"

"You started it!"

I scooped up a bigger handful of water but before I could toss it at him, he grabbed my wrist. One swift yank and he pulled me forward, straight into the tub. I crashed into his chest and ended up with my mouth conveniently pressed against his, his hand cupping the back of my neck.

Melting into him, I didn't care that I was still fully

dressed or that the tub was, indeed, too small for the both of us. When he was kissing me, nothing else mattered.

Even though my anxiety should have been reaching its zenith with Halloween literally hours away, compounded by having a deranged serial killer stalking me from beyond the grave, I was strangely ok. Between Larkin and I confessing our secrets and finally voicing our real love for each other, life was starting to look up. Maybe Halloween *was* a time for new beginnings, like Dr. Corbin said. Hopefully we'd live to see another one.

Chapter 12

Larkin

Planning the perfect, ghost-free Halloween for Jamie wasn't as easy as I'd hoped.

After the magical bath, Jamie rattled off something in Latin that was supposed to seal the deal and we proceeded to hang out like it was any other night. I kept watching him out of the corner of my eye, waiting to see if he'd suddenly tense up, the way I could now safely say was him reacting to a ghost nearby while also trying *not* to react. From what I could see, he didn't flinch at all or go strangely quiet. He was his happy, usual self. To my delighted surprise, we even messed around before falling asleep. I fully expected another ghostly wake-up call in the middle of the night, but it never came. And for the first time since *that* Halloween, Jamie woke up with a smile on his most dreaded day.

"Do you have time for breakfast?" I asked, pulling him closer and kissing his neck.

"No. My class starts in twenty."

"Want me to come with you?"

He shook his head. "Nah. I got it this year. Besides, it's right down the hall from Dr. Corbin's office. Other than that one time freshman year, no ghosts have managed to get in the classrooms when I'm around, so I think I'm good."

I blinked, watching him hop out of bed and disappear into the bathroom as if he didn't have a care in the world. I was thrilled for him, for all the progress he'd made since I brought the monster into his life, but it also meant I was more bound and determined than ever not to let anyone ruin his newfound zen or whatever the hell it was.

We left at the same time—him to go to class like the good little student he was, while I went shopping for all the things we'd need for our own version of a Halloween tradition.

And that's where the trouble began.

No matter where I went, I couldn't shake the feeling I was being watched. Not just watched. Hunted, the way the monster used to hunt for unsuspecting kids. The sick feeling churned inside of me, crawling up my spine. When it reached my neck, nearly suffocating me, I whirled around, teeth clenched, prepared to throw down with whoever was standing behind me in the cereal aisle.

No one was there.

Swallowing thickly, I snatched a box off the shelf without looking at it and carried on my way.

I turned the corner to grab some popcorn from the next aisle over when something on the floor caught my eye.

A black square, surrounded by a white border, lay on the linoleum. A polaroid. An old polaroid by the looks of it.

Someone had written something on the back in a nearly illegible script.

Carson, 9.

My stomach lurched as I turned the picture over. I barely registered a glimpse of the naked boy, crying and terrified for all eternity, before I shoved the photo in my pocket and raced to the end of the aisle. Glancing this way and that, I stared down anyone who so much as glanced in my direction. None of the shoppers paid me much attention. They were too busy picking up last-minute bags of candy and party decorations to be concerned with someone wigging out next to the display of frosted pumpkin bars.

Was I losing my mind? No. I wasn't imagining that fucking picture. Although, I couldn't help but wonder if this is what Jamie felt like every time he saw a ghost, minus the physical proof right there in his pocket.

Exhaling a breath, I pushed my cart to the checkout and left as quickly as I could.

I tried to shake off what happened with the smell of freshly-baked cookies, but the creepy feeling came back while I stood in the center of the cookie store. The place was too small for someone to lurk without me seeing them, but the feeling was there nevertheless.

I told myself I was being paranoid until I found another fucking polaroid under my windshield wiper.

Nate, 10.

Ripping the photo out, I shoved the fucking thing into my pocket without even looking at it. My focus was on searching the surrounding area, looking for any sign of the monster.

Colored leaves tumbled down the sidewalk and jack-o-lanterns grinned in the bright sun, clustered in window displays and on stoops. Winslow looked like a postcard but I knew how deceiving looks could be.

I needed to find the monster's fucking truck, then I could put an end to all of this. The last thing I needed was for that asshole ghost to drop one of these fucking pictures in Jamie's lap—or Chief Treadwell's. *That* was a story I didn't feel like explaining to anyone, no matter how sympathetic they might have been to my tragic little backstory. Jamie didn't need to see any more of the monster's handiwork and I sure as shit didn't need the police sniffing around when I was trying to get a job with them.

Climbing behind the wheel of my SUV, I pulled out into traffic and headed back to Jamie's. Was it too early to start drinking? I mean, usually, Jamie and I refrained from alcohol on Halloween but this year we could both do with a shot—or ten.

I was stopped at a light, stewing about the physics of how ghosts transported objects from Point A to Point B, when a very familiar beat-up brown truck rolled by.

"No fucking way," I muttered.

Yanking on the wheel, I pulled a U-turn in the intersection, ignoring the horns blaring behind me. The truck was right in front of me, but I still couldn't get the damn registration numbers. The hunk of rust that served as a bumper was turned downward, hanging on by a frayed twist tie, which meant I couldn't even make out what state it was from. All I could tell about the driver was that he had a bigger frame and dark hair, just like the monster.

The truck sped up, weaving around a small blue car that laid on its horn.

I stepped on the gas, darting past the same car. As we rounded a curve, I gunned it, trying to catch up to the truck before he escaped down River Road and disappeared in the countryside somewhere.

Red and blue lights lit up my rearview mirror.

"Fuck!" I slammed my hand against the steering wheel. Debating the consequences of not pulling over while trying not to lose sight of the truck, I ultimately gave up the chase with a frustrated growl and pulled to the side of the road.

License, insurance card, and registration in hand, I

rolled my window down with a huff and waited to see which officer it was. Since I'd spent the summer interning for Winslow PD, I was hoping I could bullshit my way out of a ticket.

Chief Treadwell himself stopped beside my window, eyebrows raised behind his mirrored aviators. "Galvan. What the hell do you think you're doing?"

"Uh, driving, sir?"

"Over fifty in a school zone? You in a hurry?"

I squeezed my eyes shut. "Shit. I'm sorry, chief. I didn't even realize it was a school zone. Just a lot on my mind today."

"Uh huh. Me too. You know how many kids get hit by cars today?"

"Twice as likely today over any other day of the year," I answered glumly, reciting a stat that had been drilled into us in one of my public safety classes.

"Not only that, but what school did you just zip by?"

I looked around, mapping the city in my brain. "The rich one."

"Exactly. If you're going to work here you have to know who to steer clear of and the snobby assholes who send their kids to King Street Academy would love nothing more than a lawsuit. They don't need the money. They do it for fun. They also run this town, remember?" He rolled his shoulders back, his gun belt creaking. "What's with the truck?"

"Huh?" I figured it was best to play dumb, even though those sick photos were practically burning a hole in my pocket, screaming for the chief to have me step out for a random pat down.

"That piece of shit you were trying to catch up with. This a road rage thing?"

Oh shit... so he *had* realized what I was doing. This

wasn't just about kids' safety then, or lecturing me on whose ass to kiss once I was sworn in at Winslow PD.

"Thought I knew them," I said quickly, trying to shrug nonchalantly.

"I see." Even though I couldn't see his eyes, I was fairly certain he was squinting at me, assessing whether or not I was being remotely honest.

After a moment, he patted my door. "Watch the speed, Galvan. And be careful tonight. Got a feeling it's going to be crazier than usual."

"What makes you say that?"

He looked around slowly, surveying the quiet little town like he was seeing past the perfection to something else, something he didn't want to name out loud. "Call it a gut feeling."

With that, he walked back to his squad. He didn't bother waiting for me before he pulled out into traffic again and turned off his lights, leaving me gaping after him on the side of the road.

Thrilled as I was not to get a ticket or be caught with felonious photos in my pants, I couldn't help the sense of dread Treadwell's parting words inspired. I was already on edge and that just made it ten times worse.

All things considered, the truck could wait. I needed to get back to Jamie's before he got home and the fucking monster's ghost wallpapered his apartment with trophies.

"Are you ok?" Jamie asked approximately two seconds after he walked in the door, his blue eyes darting around the living room as I stopped pacing.

"Have you seen him today?"

"No. Why?"

"Just had this weird feeling..."

"What kind of feeling?" He snagged me by my pockets and tugged me forward but from the way his brows furrowed, I knew he felt the polaroids. "What is—"

I grabbed his wrist and held him in place, just in case he got the idea to pull them out. "I don't want to lie to you, but I don't want to show you either."

Worry creased his forehead. "Ok... can you tell me something about it?"

"Someone left these for me today. In town. They're pictures *he* took."

"Of...? You?"

"No. Other kids."

"And you think it was him?"

"I know it was. How else would these have gotten here?"

"Well, I haven't seen him since the other night when he —" He cleared his throat and looked away. "And he's not here now."

I let out a breath, trying to give myself an internal pep talk before I ended up being the one to ruin Jamie's day. "Let's just forget about him, if possible."

"Sounds good to me." He slipped his arms around my waist and hugged me tightly. I buried my face in his neck and closed my eyes, letting the tension ease out of my body.

As the day wore on, we fell into our usual Halloween ritual by eating an assortment of snack foods that in no way should have gone together and watching a variety of movies from a pile of pillows and blankets on the floor. Jamie was safe, curled against me with his head on my shoulder. Inside his apartment, it wasn't Halloween, it was just another day in October. The world outside, and all its monsters, ceased to exist.

Except, it didn't.

The sun set outside the windows and the sound of Winslow children storming the streets in search of candy could be heard as they cut across campus to get from one neighborhood to another—the one downside of Tennebrose being smack-dab in the middle of Winslow. The perk of staying at Jamie's, however, was getting out of the trick-or-treat headache. Kids might not have been banging on the frat house door, but plenty of Tennebrose coeds wandered over there in search of free alcohol and more. I didn't know who was more obnoxious.

But at Jamie's, it was all quiet on the Homefront. We were so unaccustomed to the little tyrants demanding candy tribute that we both jumped about a foot in the air when someone knocked on the door.

"I got it," I said as Jamie slid his legs out of my lap, allowing me to stand.

Jamie paused the movie, glancing between me and the door warily. Ghosts didn't knock, right? Maybe it was Dr. Corbin making a house call. Or the building's security guard doing a headcount or something.

Steeling myself for whatever it was, I opened the door.

No one was there.

There was, however, another polaroid.

This one was newer and showed a different handwriting on the back.

Jamie, 22.

I flipped it over. My mouth ran dry despite the cold sweat breaking out across my skin.

It *was* Jamie—*my* Jamie—clothed and asleep in a bed. I squinted at the bedding he was laying on. It was mine. Someone took this in *my* fucking room!

As soon as I heard Jamie get up and head in my direction, I hurried to hide the photo.

"What is that?" he asked, right as I slid it into my back pocket.

"Nothing. Just a prank or something."

He leaned past me and took something off the door.

Another polaroid had been taped there and like a dumbass, I'd been too focused on the one on the ground. Thank fucking God the one in Jamie's hand wasn't another kid or Jamie himself. It was Grandma's house, of all places, but the message on the back was clear.

YOU HAVE UNTIL MIDNIGHT

"Or what?" Jamie asked, his blue eyes wide.

"Or he'll kill us both."

We exchanged a long look, silently weighing our options before we acquiesced at the same time with matching sighs.

"I'll drive," I said, forcing the words out with a grimace.

Chapter 13

Jamie

The drive to Sunderland was quiet and blessedly uneventful. Or maybe I was too distracted by the unknown situation we were heading into that I didn't notice any real ghosts drifting along with the ghouls and goblins as they swarmed across quaint towns with their bags and pillowcases.

Even after the landscape changed from suburbia to rural towns, growing ever more remote, I still didn't see any sign of *him*.

"Should we call Dr. Corbin?" Larkin asked.

I shook my head. "I don't think he can help with this."

"It's a ghost, right? Isn't that his thing?"

"He said it was complicated because of the link *he* has to us."

"But that's what I don't get. We both did the magical bath. So why is *he* still haunting us?"

"Maybe the attachment is to your grandma's house since that's where he died, and that's why it didn't work."

Larkin glanced my way. "Does that mean we have to figure out how to give the house a bath now?"

"Maybe. Salt might work. I guess there's always fire."

"I'd rather *not* go to prison for arson, thanks."

"Is that worse than dismembering a body?" I raised my brows at him.

"Wow. Didn't think you'd stoop so low, Kincaid." He kept his tone light but it didn't erase the tightness at the corners of his eyes.

I took his hand and squeezed it gently. "That's not what I meant. I'm on your side. I'm just trying to put it in perspective so we can think this through. If we can't get rid of his body, getting rid of the house might be the only way to stop him. He's leaving you creepy mementos. He almost drowned me. It won't be long before he does something even worse. From my understanding, the longer he lingers in this world, the stronger he gets."

"Do you have your magic rocks?"

I reached into the backseat and grabbed the bag of crystals and herbs, rooting through it. "Yep. And I brought something for you too." I pulled out a sprig of lavender with a smirk.

He rolled his eyes. "Gee. Thanks."

"If it helps, then you should try it."

"I've seen enough of that psycho to last a lifetime. I don't need to see any more of him."

"You might. If something happens to me, you'll need to be able to get away from him."

It was his turn to squeeze my hand, kissing the back of it. "I won't let anything happen to you."

I wanted to believe him, but as the sign for Sunderland came into view, I felt less and less certain that I'd live to loathe another Halloween.

"Where are you going?" I asked as Larkin drove past his grandmother's house and literally hopped the curb at the end of the street to drive out into the cornfield. An army of dry, yellowed stalks stood tall and unharvested, providing plenty of cover from prying eyes.

"I'm not leaving my car in plain view of the house, in case we do end up torching it," Larkin replied.

No witnesses. Made sense. Although, I couldn't help but wonder how long it would be before our corpses were discovered after we were murdered by a killer ghost in the middle of a field.

On our way through the corn, I clung to the back of Larkin's jacket, partly so I didn't trip over the tangle of stalks and partly out of sheer cowardice. Cornfields were always creepy, but especially in the fall. Their golden stalks turned brown and scratched against each other, like greedy monsters rubbing their skinny hands together in delight, just waiting to snatch unsuspecting children and drag them deep into the dark earth. It didn't help when you could hear things rustling all around you or when those dried-out husks snapped under the weight of something you couldn't see.

Larkin pulled up short before we'd even reached the edge of the field, swearing under his breath.

"What's wrong?"

"His fucking truck!" Without elaborating, he hurried over to the tree line separating his grandma's house from the field and yanked bundles of dried stalks away from where it was more or less camouflaging a beat-up pickup.

While he ripped open the door and started tearing apart the interior, for what I had no idea, I wandered closer to the front and laid my hand on the hood.

"The engine is warm," I said, casting a cautious glance around us. When Larkin didn't respond, I walked over to the cab and smacked his bicep. "Ghosts don't drive, Larkin."

"I'm telling you, he's fucking dead," Larkin snapped, climbing out of the cab with an old plastic shopping bag wrapped around something hard, like a large book. "I butchered his miserable body like the fucking animal he was and dumped him for the coyotes to eat."

"Then who is driving his truck? And those pictures you keep finding? Yeah, it could have been him, but I'm starting to think there's more than a ghost behind this."

Larkin's eyes widened, but he wasn't looking at me anymore. He was looking past me with an expression I'd never seen on his face—one of real fear.

Holding my breath, I turned slowly, trying to prepare for the worst.

The horror my brain conjured wasn't even close to reality.

A ghost had emerged from the middle of the cornfield behind us, its long white sheet caressing each stalk it passed with a whispering scrape. Its black eyeholes were fixated on us like a missile and each step brought us closer together.

Except ghosts didn't wear sheets.

And ghosts didn't carry guns.

I backed up slowly to Larkin, the warmth of his body only a mild comfort with a gun pointed right at us. "Lark?"

"It's going to be ok," he whispered, his hand resting on my hip, subtly pulling me closer to him.

"Fucking faggots," the ghost snarled. The man beneath

ripped the sheet off and threw it to the ground in disgust. "I didn't think you limp dicks were ever going to show."

It was Tim, one of the guys from Larkin's frat. Fury and confusion warred inside of me. Was this all a fucking prank? Some sort of reverse hazing? Part of me hoped so, but with the hostility on Tim's face, I had a feeling this was something else entirely.

"You're fucking disgusting," Tim continued, his glare drifting from me to Larkin. "I will *never* understand why Alan wanted you back so goddamn bad."

I shot a quick glance at Larkin, looking for some clue as to what this was all about. And who the hell was Alan?!

"What's your name?" Larkin asked. The fear from earlier had dissipated, replaced with a relative calm despite our situation.

"You don't even remember my fucking name?! I've been living with you since August, you self-centered asshole!" Tim screeched.

Larkin shook his head. "Your name's not Tim. Not really. He called me Ethan when I was with him. But that's not my name. So what's your real name? What did your parents call you?"

"You killed my fucking parent," Tim said, teeth bared, driving the gun toward Larkin before he drew up short, just out of reach. It didn't escape my attention that his finger was already on the trigger. "Alan was all I had and he didn't fucking want me because of you! But it doesn't matter now. I'm here to finish what he started. *Me*. Not you!"

Suddenly, everything clicked into place. Larkin's dad must have abducted Tim after he abandoned Larkin in New Mexico and now this kid had a sick attachment to a fucking monster. So much so that he was willing to kill two innocent people to avenge him.

"He's the reason," I said to Larkin. "Tim is why *he's* still here."

"Great," Larkin sighed. "Now what are we supposed to do?"

"Shut the fuck up! That's what you can do!" Tim shouted. I vaguely wondered if any of the neighbors would hear him, but I doubted it. All of the trick-or-treaters had gone home. Most everyone in Sunderland was probably asleep by now.

"What do you want from us? Huh?" Larkin shot back, dropping the empathetic approach. He took a step forward, practically blocking me with his frame, while he spread his arms impatiently. "Alan is gone. Ok? He's dead and he's never coming back for you. So you can spend the rest of your life crying over it or you can go find your real family and leave me the fuck alone!"

Tim laughed bitterly. "You know, he had this plan. He couldn't wait until I was old enough to get into Tennebrose, so I could get close to you. Be your friend. Convince you to give him another chance. He wanted you to be the one to carry on what he started, pick up where you two left off in New Mexico. But then your fucking grandmother died and he couldn't wait anymore.

"He thought she was the only thing that would stop you, even though I told him all about Jamie here. How fucking devoted you were. Like a lovesick puppy. You might have played it off as friendship, but I knew better. I can spot faggots like you from a mile away, which is why I couldn't believe Alan would even want you back. You turned out to be *everything* he hated. Everything he tried to wipe out of this world."

Larkin scoffed. "Trust me. He only wanted me because I got away. He didn't love me and he sure as fuck didn't love you. The only thing he cared about was inflicting as much pain as possible on people. So what did he do to you? Were you bait, too? Did you help him kidnap those other kids? It's better them than you, right? As long as you help him, you're safe. At least from being killed.

"What did he do when he caught you crying? I know you cried. Did he call you a little *fag*? A fucking fairy princess? Or how about when you tried to run away? Bet you only tried once. He broke my leg the first time I did it. Hit me so hard with a metal pipe that he broke my femur. Then he threw me into a crawl space with a dead body as punishment. I don't know about you, but I preferred the crawl space to sleeping in his bed."

Tim and I winced at the same time. I reached out slowly, curling my fingers around Larkin's and squeezing, as much to comfort him as it was to comfort myself. I didn't want to hear anymore. I didn't want to picture what that despicable fiend had done to my best friend—or anyone.

But now that he was getting under Tim's skin, Larkin wasn't stopping and he wasn't pulling any more punches. "I know he touched you. When the cops were too close and he had to lay low, he had to get off somehow between the kills. Did he make you touch him, too? Tell you how fucking filthy you were the whole time? What a *fag* you were? How you were lucky he came along when he did, because no one else would ever love you? You're too disgusting to love. Too fucking broken. A broken little toy made for *his* amusement, to play with whenever he wants."

"Shut the fuck up!" Tim said through his teeth, adjusting his grip on the pistol.

"You were with him for a long time, weren't you? Yeah. Just look at you." Larkin snorted in disgust and took a step forward, his shoulders pushed back and the gun right in front of him. "A mini fucking Alan in the making. Did he make you touch the other boys too? Or just watch while he did it? Do you still see them? Hear their screams? Did he teach you to kill? How to draw it out as long as you can? I'm guessing not, otherwise you wouldn't be standing over there hiding behind a gun like a fucking pussy. You'd be over here with your hands wrapped around my throat, showing me what a *man* you are. What are you afraid of? Hmm? A couple of *fags* like us couldn't possibly fight off a *man* like you. So come on! Show us what he taught you! Show us how *manly* you are!"

A silver light appeared behind Tim. Alan, the monster of our childhood, came into view, sneering at us from his protege's side.

"He's here!" I shouted. "Larkin, he's here!" It had the intended effect. Tim glanced away for a split second, probably trying to see what I was talking about. Larkin lunged for him.

I fumbled for the slip of paper from Dr. Corbin, yanking it out of my pocket and trying to read it with my phone's flashlight. The incantation was long and in Latin, so I stumbled over the words even though I already recited it the night before. It didn't help that I lost my place every time I glanced at Tim and Larkin, cringing as they traded blows and wrestled over the gun.

Before I could finish the arcane paragraph, the wind ripped the paper out of my hand. The wind—or a ghost.

I snatched at the air, but the paper fluttered away as a cold pressure enveloped me from behind, squeezing the air out of my lungs.

"Miss me, Jamie?" the monster's voice hissed in my ear.

"I told you I was going to kill you, you little bitch. And then I'm going to kill your fucking boyfriend, unless Tim gets to him first."

I was dimly aware of the silvery light surrounding me, crushing me, as I dropped to my knees, fighting to take a breath, however small.

"Jamie!" Larkin yelled. A sickening punch slammed into his jaw, sending him sprawling onto his back.

This was it. This was how we would die. On Halloween, in Sunderland, at the hands of the monster who tried nine years ago. At least Larkin and I were together. That was the only silver lining as my vision faded at the edges.

Larkin wasn't down for long. He scrambled to his feet as I wheezed helplessly a few feet away from him, immobilized by an invisible, icy force and the unseen hands crushing my windpipe.

Tim took aim at Larkin and squeezed the trigger. Larkin screamed, collapsing. But somewhere in the background, someone else screamed too. I was sure of it. It was a woman's voice, a shrieking mix of fear and ferocity and anger.

In the next instant, a bright light shot across the dark field, straight toward me. Blinding what was left of my view, the light engulfed me. As quickly as it started, it was over. The silver light and cold pressure evaporated into nothingness.

No longer held in the clutches of the spectral grasp, I crashed to the ground next to Larkin, coughing and gasping for air. Larkin stretched his hand toward me, his breathing labored. I managed to graze his fingers with mine as Tim took another step closer.

"Fucking fags. This is what you all deserve," Tim

growled, aiming at Larkin again. Time slowed as he pulled the trigger.

The gun clicked.

He squeezed again.

Another useless click.

"What the fuck?!" Tim angled the gun just enough to inspect the slide and the end of the barrel. Without warning, it fired over his shoulder. He yelped and jumped. The gun fell from his hand and bounced away.

Larkin threw himself forward and grabbed it from the dirt. He didn't even hesitate, pulling the trigger again and again and again. All of the bullets found their mark, knocking Tim backward until he fell, laying motionless on the ground.

"Are you ok?" Pushing myself onto my hands and knees, I crawled over to Larkin and reached for his shoulder, yanking my hand back at the last second with a gasp. A bloom of darkness was spreading over his left shoulder, wet and glistening in the moonlight. "Oh my God! You were shot!"

"I'll live," Larkin replied with a grimace.

I yanked my jacket off and wadded it up, pressing it against the entry wound while feeling around the backside for any torn fabric to see if there was an exit. There was, which was only minimally comforting. I peeled my hoodie off too and balled it up on the ground.

"Do you still see *him* anywhere?" Larkin asked, groaning and hissing through his teeth when I pushed him onto his back to keep pressure on the exit wound too.

I surveyed the dark landscape, already shaking my head in answer to his question. I almost said "No" until I spied a ball of silver light hovering near the trees.

"Jame?" Larkin prompted warily, trying to follow my line of sight. "What is it?"

"Your grandma is here," I said quietly, beyond shocked to see her ghost. I'd been so relieved when she passed and I hadn't encountered her anywhere, either at the house or the funeral. It meant she'd moved on, and maybe she did. Maybe she was only back because of Halloween. Wasn't that what Dr. Corbin said? The Celts reunited with their relatives?

"What? Where?" Larkin hurled himself into a sitting position, searching the darkness.

Shoving him back down, I adjusted my grip on the wad of bloody cloth. "Stop moving! You could have a shattered bone in there."

"Jamie?" It was Larkin's grandma, drifting closer at a slow, cautious speed. "You can see me, can't you?"

I nodded but kept my focus on slowing the blood pouring out of Larkin's left shoulder.

"You could see Larkin's father, too." It wasn't a question, but I nodded anyway. "He's gone. Larkin's mother came and took him beyond the veil, where he can't find his way back. He won't hurt you anymore. You, or Larkin."

"Thank you," I murmured. I didn't know what she did to *him*, or how, but I had a feeling her arrival was the reason the two of us were still breathing. I'd never met Larkin's mom when she was alive, but I would make certain to pay my respects at her grave.

"For what?" Larkin asked, blinking at me.

I cleared my throat, pretending I didn't hear him.

"Can you tell Larkin something for me?" Larkin's grandma paused, waiting for another nod. "Tell him his mother and I love him, that he's *nothing* like his father. And

I'm sorry I tried to keep you two apart. I see how much you love each other. I've always seen it. It was wrong of me to force him to be something he's not. Will you tell him?"

Swallowing thickly, I gave her another nod. "I will."

"Will what?" Larkin asked, his eyes widening. "Is she still here? Talking to you?"

In answer to his question, his grandma knelt beside him and reached out, brushing his cheek with her transparent fingertips.

Larkin exhaled sharply, clutching my knee. "Grandma? Is that you? Jame, was that her?"

"Te amo, mijo," she whispered with a sad smile, fading from sight.

"She's gone now," I said softly, "but she wanted me to give you a message, if you want to hear it."

"Of course I want to hear it."

Somehow I managed to relay what she said with minimal tears and only one sniffle. While I wished Larkin could have heard her himself, or that she'd told him all of that when she was still alive, I guess it was better late than never.

Larkin looped one arm around my neck and pulled me against him, hugging me tightly. "Thank you for telling me."

After a moment of holding each other, the weight of the real world settled on my shoulders like a giant boulder. I sighed, turning my attention to Tim's lifeless body. "What are we going to do about him?"

"I suppose we should call the cops," Larkin said glumly.

"I'm surprised they're not here already, with the gunshots. You know Mrs. Koch was always bitching about how loud we were as kids."

He made a face and waved me off. "Do you know how

many noise complaints cops get on Halloween? It's like New Year's or the Fourth of July. They probably assume it's fireworks. Even if they drove down the street, they wouldn't see us out here."

"I mean... if you think they're busy, then we shouldn't add to their workload," I said slyly.

He gave me a curious look before picking up what I was putting down. "It's so much paperwork. Detectives need to be called. Along with the coroner. Not to mention the poor paramedics we'd end up waking up."

"So, really, we'd be doing everyone a favor by *not* calling it in."

He nodded solemnly. "I think so."

I nodded as well. "On one condition, though."

Larkin raised both brows, waiting.

"You go see Dr. Corbin for your shoulder as soon as we get back to Winslow."

"Considering he told us to dig up a corpse and set it on fire, I'm guessing he won't be too concerned with reporting a bullet hole to Treadwell."

"Yeah, probably not."

"Ok. First, we get rid of Tim's body and the truck, then we go see Corbin. Deal?"

"Deal. Does your grandma have salt in the house?"

He chuckled. "Oh yeah. Table. Pickling. Kosher. Take your pick."

"Ok. I'm going to go get the stuff we need to do the cleansing thing, just to be on the safe side, and I'll be right back. Do *not* move. Do you hear me?"

"Yes, sir. Sitting right here."

"Good. I'll be right back."

It didn't take long to find all of the stuff I needed inside the house and the garage and return to the scene of the crime.

Loading Tim's body into the back of the pickup wasn't easy, especially since Larkin was limited with his arm in a makeshift sling, but we managed. Following Larkin's SUV in the pickup, I drove through the field slowly, along the farmer's path until the cornfield gave way to the dark, twisting forest on the edge of the mountain.

As we set fire to Tim's salted body, I couldn't help but feel a sense of relief. Between Dr. Corbin's ritual and what Larkin's grandmother said, I knew, deep in my soul, that my would-be murderer was gone for good.

"Not the Halloween bonfire I imagined we'd have one day," Larkin said, draping his right arm over my shoulders.

"Don't be morbid." I elbowed him in the ribs. Turning back to the fully-engulfed body, I frowned. "Who was he? Really?"

"I have no idea. I'm sure he's in that scrapbook somewhere. *He* kept photos. I might be able to match one of them to a missing poster or something. Plus, there's a map of where the bodies are buried. *He* liked to reminisce when he was in the area. Sick fuck."

"What are you going to do now? Give all of that to the FBI?"

Larkin shook his head sadly. "No. They won't do anything now that he's dead. But I do want to give the families closure. I was hoping you could help with that?"

"How?"

"I've got the map and these pictures, but I don't know which dot goes with which kid. Maybe, if we went there, you could see if their ghosts are still around? Maybe see if they have a message for their families? Then we can send them a letter or something. Anonymously. So they can give their kids a proper burial or whatever. At least know the truth of what happened. Well... mostly. There are some things parents don't need to know."

I leaned into him, lifting my hand to lace my fingers through his. "Absolutely. I'll help however I can, for however long it takes."

"I don't deserve you."

"You're a good man, Larkin. You deserve to be happy."

He turned and cupped the back of my neck, kissing me gently. My heart swelled with the amount of love I had for him. From now on, I had a feeling Halloween wouldn't be so scary anymore. The ghosts of our past were truly gone and we could move forward, hopefully giving others some peace as well.

After years of hating *him* and the curse he bestowed on me, I could finally see the bright side. Even if I never saw another ghost again, being able to relay one last message from Larkin's grandma made it all worth it. He was always the one comforting me, so it was nice to return the favor, although I wished it was under better circumstances. Getting his grandma's stamp of approval was the icing on the cake.

Believe in the power of Halloween.

Thanks to Dr. Corbin, I could officially say I did.

Despite the creepy costumes and horror movies, maybe Halloween wasn't meant to be feared after all. It was a time to spend with the people you loved and there was no one I'd rather spend Halloween with than the man beside me, the one who had always been there for me, ghosts or no ghosts, and the one I would always be there for.

"Hey, Lark," I said, wrapping my arms around his neck and losing myself in the depths of his dark eyes.

"Yeah?"

"Happy Halloween."

A smile stretched across his face, dimples and all. "Happy Halloween."

THE END

No geese were harmed in
the writing of this book.

Want more Tennebrose?

Check out the other books in the Tennebrose series! They all act as standalones, but are more enjoyable when read in order, as the town's history builds on itself.

CALIGO – a short MM story about an eager grad student, his "crazy" history professor, and a trip to the woods in search of the infamous Winslow Witch. This is a newsletter exclusive.

MALUM DISCORDIAE – a dark academia, paranormal MM romance about witches, Necromancers, and a blood feud that has lasted centuries. It features plenty of steam, a lot of snark, and the pile of bodies you'd expect in a magical Romeo + Juliet retelling—except this one has a happy ending.

IGNI FERROQUE – a dark MM paranormal romance about a pious Necromancer and an incorrigible demon and what happens when their paths intersect. There's scorching steam and brutal violence in this enemies-to-lovers tale, wrapped up with plenty of intrigue and betrayal.

MORTEM OBIRE — a MM, best friends-to-lovers paranormal romance novella about ghosts, serial killers, and a deep-rooted fear of Halloween. There's a healthy dose of angst mixed in with the steamy moments between two guys who are "just friends," all the Halloween vibes, and a cameo by one very lovable goat.

Also by Ashlyn Drewek

The Leander Welles Series:

THE MYSTERY OF LEANDER WELLES — a dark, psychological romantic suspense about a criminal psychiatrist who falls in love with her patient. *Finalist for Suspense in the 2021 Next Generation Indie Book Awards.*

THE RATIONALE OF LEANDER WELLES — a dark, psychological romantic suspense about an alleged murderer who falls in love with his psychiatrist... or does he?

THE DAMNATION OF LEANDER WELLES: OR, THE DEATH & LIFE OF BENNETT REEVE — a dark MM friends-to-lovers romance about a cutthroat lawyer and an enigmatic millionaire and what happens when two dark souls join forces. *A prequel to Book 1 and 2.*

THE WRATH OF LEANDER WELLES — a dark, MM romantic suspense about love, revenge, and how far a psychopath is willing to go for both.

The Solnyshko Duet:

THE KIDNAPPING OF ROAN SINCLAIR — THE KIDNAPPING OF ROAN SINCLAIR is a dark MM mafia romance about a spoiled American who is kidnapped by a Russian criminal and their harrowing journey to survive. Welcome to a world full of angst, steam, and brutal violence.

THE VENGEANCE OF ROAN SINCLAIR — a dark MM mafia romance about love in the aftermath of trauma and finding your new normal. There are emotional steamy scenes, plenty of violence and revenge, and a much-needed HEA.

The Tennebrose Series:

CALIGO — a short MM story about an eager grad student, his "crazy" history professor, and a trip to the woods in search of the infamous Winslow Witch. This is a newsletter exclusive.

MALUM DISCORDIAE — a dark academia, paranormal MM romance about witches, Necromancers, and a blood feud that has lasted centuries. It features plenty of steam, a lot of snark, and the pile of bodies you'd expect in a magical Romeo + Juliet retelling—except this one has a happy ending.

IGNI FERROQUE — a dark MM paranormal romance about a pious Necromancer and an incorrigible demon and what happens when their paths intersect. There's scorching steam and brutal violence in this enemies-to-lovers tale, wrapped up with plenty of intrigue and betrayal.

MORTEM OBIRE — an MM, best friends-to-lovers paranormal romance novella about ghosts, serial killers, and a deep-rooted fear of Halloween. There's a healthy dose of angst mixed in with the steamy moments between two guys who are "just friends," all the Halloween vibes, and a cameo by one very lovable goat.

Paranormal & Dark Fantasy Standalones:

THE COVENTRY CAROL — a darker MM Christmas romance standalone novella. If you love Christmas and cozy Hallmark movies with all the sweet, swoony romance, this is NOT the book for you. It's heavy on Christmas folklore (i.e. dark traditions) in addition to insta-lust and steam, and a lot of triggering themes. Consider it an anti-Christmas story, if you will, that still manages to end in a HEA.

PER SANGUINEM — a slow-burn MM paranormal romance with a lot of suspense, police procedures, and sexual tension between two cops on the DL. It features an overprotective vampire, two insanely loyal partners, and a forbidden love story set against a complicated backdrop of murder and vampire politics.

Contemporary Standalones:

BRIAR & BRAMBLE — a darker Valentine's Day MM novella about a pair of grumpy/sunshine ex-stepbrothers, old wounds, and steamy second chances. This was originally published in the *Anti-Valentine* anthology and is now exclusive to my website.

WITHER — a "Beauty and the Beast"-inspired MM novella about a librarian desperate for a change, an award-winning author who hates the world, a six-month contract, and the book that will change their lives. The original version of this story was published in the

Because of You anthology and has been expanded prior to its rerelease.

About the Author

International best-selling and award-winning dark romance author Ashlyn Drewek has always been a hopeless romantic. She's also fascinated by the dark, macabre things in life such as Halloween, murder, cemeteries, and witchcraft. Not necessarily in that order.

Most of her time is spent making up stories in her head or researching obscure historical topics. The results of those efforts usually end up in a book as some sort of weird Easter egg or symbolism. Anything to make Edgar Allan Poe proud.

For information on news, upcoming releases, and where to find Ashlyn on social media, check out the QR code below.

Printed in Poland
by Amazon Fulfillment
Poland Sp. z o.o., Wrocław

40836871R00084